P9-DTO-840

ALL THE
COLORS
OF MAGIC

ALL THE COLORS OF MAGIC

VALIJA ZINCK

Chicken House

Scholastic Inc. / New York

First published in Germany in 2017 as *Penelop und der funkenrote Zauber* by S. Fischer Verlag GmbH, Frankfurt. First published in the United Kingdom in 2018 as *A Tangle of Magic* by Chicken House, 2 Palmer Street, Frome, Somerset BA11 1DS.

Library of Congress Cataloging-in-Publication Data available

ISBN 978-1-338-54061-1

10 9 8 7 6 5 4 3 2 1 19 20 21 22 23

Printed in the U.S.A. 23

First edition, December 2019

Book design by Maeve Norton

1
Penelope Gardener

Penelope Gardener was an odd sort of girl. She had gray hair, although she was only ten years old, and a smell of fire followed her wherever she went. But stranger still, Penelope could sometimes hear her mother telling her to do something before Mrs. Gardener had even opened her mouth.

"Yes, Mom, I did wash my hair this morning," Penelope would say. Or: "OK, OK, I'm taking Granny her coffee right now." Mom would look at her with a very strange expression, but never asked Penelope how she'd known exactly what she was about to say.

Penelope was used to her gray hair—she'd never known anything else. She hardly noticed the fire smell anymore, and she barely gave the hearing-before-hearing a second thought. But there was one thing that struck her as odd: It always rained on her birthday on the thirteenth of August. Hardly anyone except Penelope seemed to notice it. And because most people put an umbrella up or wore a raincoat when it rained, hardly anyone except Penelope seemed to notice that the rain on her birthday wasn't really wet.

On her seventh birthday, when Penelope had asked about the strange rain, her mother's face had turned pale. "I don't want to hear another word about peculiar stuff like that!" she'd snapped. "I've had enough of it to last me a lifetime!" Penelope had asked her what she meant, but Mrs. Gardener had stayed quiet, and Penelope thought she saw the glint of a tear in her eye. And because she loved her mother very much, she never mentioned the strange birthday rain again.

Not when it fell again on her eighth birthday, nor at any time after that.

Penelope lived with her mother, her granny Elizabeth, and their gray cat, Coco, in a small house on the outskirts of a little village, right next to a swamp forest. The house was narrow and a bit drafty, but Penelope loved it. The wooden walls were once bright red, but Penelope's mother had painted them dark green. Every year after the summer rains, a little of the green paint would flake away, and a little more red would show through. Now the house was speckled all over with red and green, like dragon scales.

Penelope's father didn't live in the dragon house. He didn't live anywhere anymore, as he'd died when Penelope was very young. She missed her father, even though she didn't remember him. The only things she had of his were Coco and a tattered old black-and-white photo that showed a long-haired man with his arms around Penelope's mother, laughing. There were no wrinkles on her mother's brow in the photo, and she had a round, expectant Penelope belly.

Apart from the photo, there was nothing in the house to remind her of her father. Mrs. Gardener had given away all of his belongings because it made her too sad to have them around. Penelope thought that was a pity. She'd have liked to have known more about her father, and his things could have told her a little bit about him. Sometimes, when Penelope asked about him, Granny would say, "It's a real shame the chap's not around anymore, isn't it?" But Penelope's mother never replied.

2

Rainy Weather

One gloomy Friday morning in April, Penelope was woken by something crawling across her nose.

"Stop it, Coco!" she murmured, still half-asleep. But then it occurred to her that the cat was lying on her feet like a hot-water bottle. Also, whatever was crawling over her face seemed to have an awful lot of legs.

She sat up with a start, the creature clinging to her cheek. "Holy swamp cow!" she shouted, reaching up and brushing the large gray-and-yellow cellar spider off her face, shuddering in disgust. "What do you think you're playing at?"

The cellar spider didn't reply, of course—it scuttled under the bed as fast as its spindly legs would carry it.

"I don't think much of your manners!" she called after it. Penelope didn't really mind leggy spiders, hairy spiders, or any creepy-crawlies, but she wasn't too keen on them strolling across her face at six in the morning. Her eyes fell on Coco, who was still sound asleep.

"Call yourself a guard cat? I get attacked by an eight-legged monster at the crack of dawn, and you just lie there snoring!"

Her father's cat didn't even open an eye. *No one wants to talk to me today*, thought Penelope. But that was about to change, as the next moment a piercing shriek echoed through the house.

"Penelopeeeee! Heeeeeeeeeelp!"

Aha! At least her mother wasn't ignoring her too. No doubt the milk had boiled over, or maybe she'd spilled the coffee. But as Penelope hurried down the worn wooden staircase, she could smell neither burnt milk nor delicious coffee, and her mother was curled up on the sofa bed, sound asleep. Penelope listened for Granny, but all she could hear was the old woman's snores drifting from her bedroom.

She sighed, realizing what had happened. That dratted hearing-before-hearing! Sometimes it could be a real pain. The "before" could be minutes or hours or even several days before—it was really confusing.

Quietly, so as not to wake her mother, she started getting breakfast ready. She set the kettle to boil for her verbena tea and buttered a bread roll. Mrs. Gardener was a clarinetist at the theater in the nearest town. When she had a show in the evening, she often didn't get home until after midnight and tended to sleep late the next morning, so Penelope would eat her breakfast alone. She tucked her gray hair behind her ears, took a bite of her roll, and watched the raindrops running down the window-pane in crinkly streams. What a pity it couldn't have been birthday rain so she could have stayed nice and dry! *I'm going to be drenched before I even get to the bus stop*, thought Penelope as she took another sip of tea.

An icy wind gusted around the red-and-green-speckled house, blowing the rain into her face as Penelope stepped outside. She ducked her head between her shoulders and went to fetch her bike from the shed. The path between the house and the road leading into the village was a bumpy sand track with herbs growing along the edges. Penelope had to push her bike along the track until she reached the old beech tree, where the road started. Here, she climbed onto her bike and pedaled up the steep hill that led into the village, where the school bus stopped.

She was halfway up when she saw a tractor cresting the top of the hill and trundling down. The tractor was a bright, mud-splattered green, and puffed noxious black fumes from its exhaust pipe. The man driving it was wearing a hood shadowing his face, but underneath Penelope spotted a glint of gold-rimmed sunglasses—in spite of the rain. Penelope knew lots of the local farmers, and she'd never seen this man or his horrible tractor—besides, he was driving way too fast. She wheeled to the side of the road. The vehicle rumbled swiftly toward the huge puddle in front of her and plowed straight through the middle of it at speed, sending up a torrent of water and sand. Penelope spluttered in disbelief. She felt like she'd just been pulled out of a dirty pond.

"You stupid boil-face!" she yelled after the tractor. "You'll get what's coming to you, believe you me—and more besides!" She wiped her face. Some day this was turning out to be. First a cellar spider on her face, and now a mud shower from a tractor!

"And you're a fat lot of help!" she said to the road. "Couldn't you have taken him round some other bend instead?"

The road didn't reply, of course. Penelope sighed and pedaled on up the hill until she reached the bus stop.

"Been for a dip in the swamp forest, have we?" asked

the bus driver, grinning, as she got on. Penelope couldn't even summon up the energy to answer.

At school, Penelope tore off her wet clothes, hung them over a cupboard door, and put on the smelly T-shirt and shorts from her gym bag instead. She'd be cold, but it was better than sitting in her wet, muddy clothes—or wearing nothing at all! She'd manage somehow—she wasn't some delicate little snowflake, after all.

But when the sound of her teeth chattering disturbed Mr. Potts's lesson so much that he drew a jagged line on the whiteboard instead of a straight one, the teacher finally exclaimed: "Enough of this clattering! Boys and girls of 5B, you must lend your support. Not only to help me, your poor math teacher, but also for the sake of our dear Miss Gardener. Who will lend her a protective layer to help spare her from catching pneumonia?"

He'd have been better off asking who *wouldn't*, as everyone was only too happy to help Penelope. Soon she was resplendent in a silky vest, a mint-green polo, a hoodie, a knitted sweater, a red-and-black-striped scarf, a slightly scratchy pair of tights, a violet hair bow, a headband, a rose-patterned silver ring, and beige leggings.

"All we need now is some shoes," said Mr. Potts. He wasn't serious, but immediately two spindly boys with straw-colored hair leapt up from the table at the back. Tom and Pete were Penelope's best friends, and they were so alike they could have been identical twins: They had the same gap in their teeth, the same smile, and the same shocking blue sneakers, which they now held out to Penelope: a size 6 for her left foot and a size 7 for the right.

"We can hop till tomorrow!" shouted Pete, dropping his shoe on Penelope's desk and hopping back to his seat, arm in arm with Tom. The whole class laughed.

As Penelope slipped on the shoes, she found she was totally speechless. OK, so she was sweating in all the clothes, and the shoes were much too big for her, but what did that matter? She felt so grateful!

By the time school finished, she could have changed back into her own clothes—they were still muddy, but at least they were almost dry. But she kept her classmates' things on anyway. She wanted to hold on to the comforting feeling of being wrapped up in their friendship for as long as she could.

3

In the Swamp Forest

Outside, the heavy rain had given way to a fine drizzle, and Penelope decided it was dry enough to cycle the twelve-minute shortcut through the swamp forest.

If you have ever traveled through a swamp forest, you will know that the few paths are extremely narrow, and that you mustn't stray from them under any circumstances. Wander off, and you might find yourself sinking into the cold swamp. And then, if you manage to pull yourself out again, the boggy ground will suck the shoes from your feet and they'll be swallowed whole, never to be seen again. You'll have to walk the rest of your journey in socks!

The path was so slippery today, that as Penelope carefully steered her bike over a gnarled tree root, the tires almost skidded out from under her. She wondered if she ought to have taken the road, after all. Gripping the handlebars more tightly, she clenched her toes to keep the large sneakers on her feet—the blue shoelaces were loosening, and one of them was flapping in the wind. She steered with extreme caution around the next tree, and then stopped, startled.

There was something lying across the path in front of her, something that didn't belong in the swamp forest. A piece of dark green fabric with pink roses on it, which Penelope recognized immediately: It was one of her mother's scarves.

What the heck is that doing here? she wondered. Penelope dismounted, leaning her bike against a tree, and picked up the scarf. She scanned the forest. There was nothing out of the ordinary. Trees and swamp grass swayed in the wind, which tugged gently at her gray hair.

"Mom?" she called softly. "Are you there?"

No reply. Penelope stuffed the scarf in the pocket of the sweater. She looked all around her again, mounted her bike, and continued on her way as fast as the wet path allowed.

Penelope reached the dragon house and knocked on the green-and-red-speckled front door with numb fingers, but no sounds came from inside.

"Mom!" Penelope shouted. "Granny! Can you let me in, please?"

No reply.

Penelope walked around the house and looked through the window, feeling more worried. No pans simmered on the stove, no Mrs. Gardener practicing the clarinet, no Granny Elizabeth poring over her coin collection. Just Coco the gray cat, lying curled up on an armchair.

What's going on? thought Penelope. She sat down on the small wooden steps outside the front door and her tongue began to click against the roof of her mouth of its own accord. Penelope clicked whenever she was thinking hard. It was pretty annoying, but she couldn't help it.

"Oh, thank heavens, child, there you are!"

Suddenly, Granny Elizabeth was standing in front of her. Penelope could tell it was Granny Elizabeth by her threadbare olive-green raincoat and her plump belly, but her grandmother's face was completely different. Her skin was gray, her brown-dyed hair was in disarray, her eyes were swollen, and her nose was red. Whatever could have happened?

"Your mother's had an accident." Granny Elizabeth sank down onto the steps next to Penelope. "I've just come back from the hospital."

"What?!" Penelope jumped to her feet.

"Calm down, calm down. She's going to be fine. We can go and visit her now."

On the long bus journey to the hospital, Granny

Elizabeth explained that Penelope's mom had been knocked down by a tractor in the village. Penelope's tongue clicked. Was this the same vehicle that had soaked her on her way to school? She wasn't surprised it had hit someone—the driver was a lunatic.

"She's broken a rib and hit her head quite badly," said Granny, sighing. "And although the doctors expect her to recover fully, she's only able to stay awake for a few minutes at a time before losing consciousness again. She'll be in the hospital for a good few weeks, my dear."

"Was Mom"—*click*—"in the forest today too?"

"No," said Granny Elizabeth. "Why do you ask?"

"Because . . . Oh, nothing. I just wondered," said Penelope, feeling the scarf in the top pocket of the woolen sweater. She gazed out of the window over the meadows, toward the forest.

4

New Hair

Over the next few weeks, Penelope missed her mother terribly. She visited during the weekends, but it wasn't easy. The bus journey to the hospital took over two hours, and her mother slept a lot at first, even when Penelope was at her bedside. When she was awake, she would smile bravely at Penelope and say, "Don't worry, my love. I'm already feeling much stronger, and I'll be home soon."

Penelope hoped that was true—not only because she missed her mom, but also because Granny

Elizabeth's idea of cooking was, well, quite hard to stomach. *Cooking* wasn't the right word to describe Granny's liver dumplings (dried out from being kept in the cupboard too long), fried eggs (charred until they were almost black), or any of the other delicacies she cobbled together.

Recipe: Fried eggs à la Elizabeth Burke

Ingredients:

two eggs

a frying pan

a selection of old coins

Break the eggs into a cold frying pan without adding oil or butter. Place the pan on the stove (heat setting: highest) and start sorting the coins. Wait until the kitchen is completely filled with smoke, then turn off the stove and open the window with a loud screech. Wait until the charred eggs are stone cold, then serve.

Enjoy!

Another thing Penelope had learned recently was that it was really hard to get hold of bright blue shoelaces. The one from the sneaker Pete had lent her had disappeared—Penelope reckoned it had probably ripped out when she was in the swamp forest. Pete said she didn't need to replace it, as he had an orange shoelace he could use instead, but for Penelope, that wasn't the point. If she borrowed something, she gave it back, even if it took her a while.

At last, one Friday afternoon, the doctor at the hospital said Mrs. Gardener could go home the next day. Penelope was lying in bed that evening, tired but too excited to sleep, when she suddenly became aware that there was something missing. *Something that's always been here has gone*, she thought. But she couldn't put her finger on what it was. She switched on the little lamp that stood on her bedside table and looked around. The table with the curved legs stood under the window as usual, the rust-brown armchair was in its usual place, the wardrobe obviously hadn't gone missing, and it couldn't be the bed, either, as she was in it.

Perhaps it's something that's too small to see, thought Penelope, yawning. *But I can find out in the morning. Time to sleep now.* She turned the light off again and didn't give it any more thought. She was already half-asleep when Coco slunk into the room, jumped up onto the bed, and burrowed under the duvet, but the cat crept out again a moment later. She tapped Penelope on the nose with a furry paw and started sniffing at the air. Penelope opened her eyes blearily.

"That's it! The fire smell! I don't smell of fire anymore!"

Coco continued to tap her on the nose in distress.

"Stop it, Coco," grunted Penelope, pushing the cat aside. Coco mewed in protest, but crept back under the duvet. Feeling the cat's comforting warmth on her feet, Penelope allowed herself to slide into the land of dreams.

If a person has smelled of fire all their life, it's a little confusing when that smell disappears overnight. But Penelope felt even more confused the next morning, because when she went into the bathroom, she found a strange girl staring back at her from the mirror above the sink. The girl in the mirror had Penelope's small nose, Penelope's dark green eyes, and Penelope's pale skin, but she didn't have limp gray strands sprouting from her head—she had a wild tangle of hair as red as fire.

"Who are *you*?" Penelope asked the girl in the mirror. The girl didn't reply. Penelope pulled a strand of hair across her face; it was bright red. She blinked. The red-haired girl blinked too.

"Impossible," she murmured. The mirror-girl said nothing, but Penelope saw her lips move at the same time as her own. She sat down on the closed lid of the toilet and tried to breathe calmly. She counted to ten three times, as she often did when she needed to calm herself, but this morning it didn't help at all. *Click-click*... Her tongue had started clicking madly.

What was going on? She no longer smelled of fire—but instead she had flame-red hair. How was that possible? And what did it mean?

Suddenly, Penelope missed her mother more than ever. She wanted to throw herself into her mother's arms and lay an ear against her chest, listening to the heartbeat, the way she'd done as a small child. She wanted her mom to stroke her new red hair and say, "Penny, my Penny, you're my daughter—you smell good to me no matter what! And whether your hair's gray or red doesn't change what's on the inside."

But that was exactly it! Penelope wasn't so sure that nothing *had* changed inside her. Yes, she realized, she really did feel completely different from usual: incredibly light, and somehow permeable, and much more alert. In fact, she could sense an incredible strength in the center of her being, blazing a trail up her spine. It wasn't a bad feeling, but Penelope wasn't used to it, so it scared her a little.

Coco slunk into the bathroom, looked at Penelope, and wound herself around her legs. Penelope stooped to stroke the old cat's gray fur, wiping a tear from her cheek with her other hand. She was glad Coco was there. The cat nudged Penelope's hand hard with her nose, which meant that she was hungry, and that Penelope should kindly go downstairs and shake some biscuits into her bowl.

"It's OK, sweetie pie." Penelope straightened up and took a deep breath, wiping the last of the tears from her eyes. OK, then! If Coco could act as if this was a perfectly normal morning, then she could too.

5

Post

Filled with new determination, Penelope picked up her comb and dragged it through her new red hair, wincing as the tangles snagged and pulled. Never mind! She abandoned the comb, washed her face with cold water, and ran downstairs.

Granny wasn't up yet—probably sleeping in, as usual. Coco meowed in annoyance, and Penelope obediently shook cat food into the bowl. She set the kettle to boil and spooned verbena leaves into the teapot. What next? Today was Saturday: no school, thank goodness. And Granny wasn't collecting Mom from the hospital until late afternoon. Penelope was full of energy—she couldn't spend her day waiting around inside. She felt an urge to go outdoors—to the forest or the stone circle, or even just for a run across the fields.

She was pouring the hot water into the teapot when there was a knock at the front door.

"Come in, it's open," called Penelope. The next moment, the postman was standing in the dragon house.

"I have a delivery for the esteemed Mrs. Elizabeth Burke." He put down a large parcel and wiped a hand over his brow. Penelope smiled in sympathy—Granny's enormous coin collection never stopped growing. "Well, I'd better be on my way. Oh, and that's a very pretty hair color, by the way. A little daring, but pretty." And then he was gone.

Penelope's senses tingled.

"Haven't you forgotten something?" she called after him. "A letter? In a dark envelope?"

"What?" The postman turned. "Not that I know of." But he started to rummage through his sack anyway. Sure enough, a dark gray envelope surfaced.

"Holy mackerel! How did you know that?" His forehead crinkled in puzzlement, but Penelope just shrugged. He passed the letter to her quickly and was off outside to his van.

This letter is from someone like me, thought Penelope, and her tongue clicked. What exactly "someone like me" meant, she had no idea, but somehow she knew that whatever was in the letter, it wasn't good.

A printed sticker on the front read, *To Lucia and Penelope Gardener.* Another sticker on the back read: *Sender: L. Gardener.*

L. Gardener? Who on earth was that? Penelope had no other relatives except for a great-uncle, and his name was Ben Herbert.

"OK," Penelope said to herself, setting down her tea. "So I'll open it, and then I can find out a bit more about this L. Gardener." But then she paused. Her mother might not want her to read this letter, and Penelope didn't like the idea of upsetting her. But what was the problem? It was addressed to her, too, after all!

"I'll just take a quick look," she said to herself, and

held the envelope over the still-steaming kettle. "I can stick it back together again afterward, and Mom will never know."

Coco mewed, arched her back, and swished her tail through the air as if she was afraid.

"Calm down," Penelope said, frowning at the cat. "I don't think any wild dogs are going to jump out of it!" The flap of the envelope loosened, and she peered inside.

What was this? No letter. No card either. The envelope contained just one thing: a five-dollar bill.

"Hmm," said Penelope. "What *is* this?"

"Pennyyyyy!" A shrill voice resounded through the house. Granny Elizabeth was standing on the wooden staircase. Her face was as white as her linen nightdress. Hastily, Penelope stuck the envelope closed and shoved it under the heavy parcel.

But Granny wasn't looking at the letter. "Your hair! Oh, good heavens, child, your hair!" She was staring at Penelope as though a stranger was standing in the kitchen, not her granddaughter. Penelope was confused—and then she remembered: She had red hair now. In all her puzzlement over the gray letter, she'd completely forgotten!

Penelope tossed her new red curls over her shoulder, determined to be brave. "My hair looks pretty. Well, the postman thought so anyway. Do you want a cup of tea?"

"You mean someone's seen you like that?" cried her grandmother, clutching the banister in horror. "Oh, my goodness!"

Suddenly, Penelope felt very cross: She couldn't believe how Granny was reacting! *Granny sleeps till all hours*, she thought, *and when she finally surfaces, all she can do is pick a fight. She could at least have asked me how I actually* feel *about this, and*... Unable to bear it, she stamped her foot so hard on the wooden floor that dust billowed into the air.

Granny's face had set into an expression of determination to match Penelope's. "That red tangle is coming off *right now*. Sit down, and I'll get the scissors," she said, and turned toward the bathroom.

“Are you crazy?” Penelope shouted at her granny’s retreating back. Now she was *really* angry. “Cut off whatever you want, but not my beautiful new hair!” And she raced outside, the door crashing violently against the side of the dragon house.

Penelope ignored Granny’s screeches of protest and stumbled down the steps. She tore across the meadow, heading for the forest, nearly tripping into a ditch in her haste to run as far away as possible. A deer emerged as Penelope reached the first line of trees, glancing at her curiously, but she didn’t even notice. She raced over the dew-soaked woodland grass as if she were flying, as if her feet were airborne, touching neither grass nor earth beneath her. A fiery tail of hair streamed out in her wake, glowing in the sunlight like red gold.

A Gray Homecoming

Darkness was falling by the time Penelope returned to the dragon house. It was dark and empty, and Penelope felt suddenly worried. But of course, she realized, Granny Elizabeth was collecting Mom from the hospital. On the kitchen table, propped against the open package of old coins, stood a note on yellow paper:

We'll be back very late,
you might as well go to bed.

Regards, G. E.

Regards, G.E.? What sort of tone is that? Not a friendly one, at any rate, thought Penelope as she cut herself a thick slice of onion bread and drank huge gulps of water from the tap. Oh, well, never mind—tomorrow, at last, her mother would be home. She would stroke Penelope's hair and braid it into two red plaits; then they'd go off to the forest hand in hand—Granny Elizabeth (or G.E., as she seemed to be calling herself now) could stay at home, cut up her linen nightie with her precious scissors, pore over her coin collection, and be as unfriendly as she liked. That was absolutely fine as far as Penelope was concerned.

She went into the bathroom to wash—she was quite grubby after her day spent outside. But after rinsing her hands and face, she simply stood in front of the mirror for a long time, gazing at her hair. How shiny it was, and how soft it felt! It was like a huge, curly red veil that enveloped and protected her, hugging her shoulders and flowing down her back. It'd been such a shock when she'd first seen it in the mirror, only this morning, but now she couldn't even imagine that she'd ever looked any different. She felt light and free. The strange power she'd felt blazing inside her that morning had settled into a peaceful humming sensation.

Coco wandered into the bathroom and started to climb up Penelope's leg. "OK, I'm coming," laughed Penelope, following the old cat over the creaky floorboards into her room and into bed.

Just as she was dropping off to sleep, she heard the front door open. Mom was home!

She jumped up and raced out of the room—but paused on the landing. Her mother's voice was raised and angry. Penelope could hear her pacing up and down the kitchen floor with quick footsteps. "Only five dollars, you said? Unbelievable. Is he trying to taunt me now, after everything he's put me through? What's that about? Can you explain it to me, Mother? That blasted man, if only I'd never—"

"Then you wouldn't have Penelope," Granny Elizabeth pointed out, in a softer tone. "And she's your everything—you're always saying so. Besides, he was the love of your life. Hindsight is everything, as they say, but you weren't to know how things would end up."

Silence, apart from the ticking of the kitchen clock. Penelope frowned in the half-light of the landing. What were they talking about? What "blasted man"? What "love of her life"? And what did all that have to do with the five dollars?

"Oh, and—" Granny Elizabeth broke off. "No, on second thought, now that you've got yourself so worked up, I'm not going to tell you."

"Tell me what?" Her mother's voice sounded shrill now.

Granny was silent.

Mom's voice was deadly serious. "Tell. Me. What? *Mother*..." There was a sharp note of warning in her voice.

Granny sighed. "Well, it's... it's Penelope's hair. It seems to have taken on a bit of a reddish tone—not that strong, she barely noticed it herself—but you really should—"

"Oh, for heaven's sake!" cried her mother. "It sounds

like I got out of the hospital just in time, or we really would have had a disaster on our hands!"

Disaster? What disaster? For the second time that day, Penelope felt angry. She'd thought her mother would be happy about her hair, and now to hear her say something like that . . . ! Yes, the abrupt change was odd—but what was wrong with red hair? Suddenly, she felt very alone. The urge to storm downstairs quickly deserted her, and she felt a lump forming in her throat. She crept back to bed and pulled the duvet up to her nose. A wild hubbub of voices pounded in her head: *. . . Then you wouldn't have Penelope . . . He was the love of your life . . . That blasted man . . .*

Could they have been talking about her father? *L. Gardener*, the sticker on the envelope had said. Could that be *Leo* Gardener? Leo Arthur, that had been her father's name. But her father was dead—so how could he taunt her mother? Penelope's tongue was clicking so hard that the roof of her mouth had started to hurt. And why was G.E. talking about a "bit of a reddish tone"? Had she suddenly gone color-blind? It would be impossible to find a redder head of hair than Penelope's!

She heard footsteps on the stairs. Penelope turned to face the wall. She didn't want to see anyone—but her mouth was clicking wildly, and she knew her mother or G.E. would hear. She'd have to stop it right away.

Don't think about it. Think about something else, thought Penelope. *Something boring, think about something boring. White mushrooms, field mushrooms, horse mushrooms . . .* click, click. *Toadstools, puffballs, truffles . . .* click. The footsteps grew closer and stopped in front of her bedroom door. *Porridge, cheese sandwiches, sugar-free jam . . .* The latch was pressed downward. *Dandelions, dock leaves, thistles, weeds.*

Success! Penelope's tongue tapped one more time, lightly, against the roof of her mouth, and then was still.

Her bedroom door opened, and Mrs. Gardener crept into the dark room. "Penelope, love?"

Penelope didn't answer, but kept her eyes closed and tried to breathe as quietly as possible. Her mother sat down on the bed and sighed softly. After a moment, she started to stroke Penelope's hair. Penelope felt her muscles relax. She'd really missed her mom! She could almost forget that she'd ever been angry with her.

Snap!

Penelope stiffened. Was that the sound of a lid being opened? A strange and very familiar smell—a smell like fire—floated up to Penelope's nostrils; then she felt her hair being stroked again. But it felt different now. It wasn't her mother's hand anymore—it was an object of some kind. Something cold and hard, like a spatula . . . Penelope sat up and snapped the light on.

"What are you doing?" Penelope asked.

Mrs. Gardener froze, her mouth open in shock. In her hand was a dripping paintbrush and in her lap sat a large glass bowl, bubbling with gray paste. Penelope sniffed: The familiar stench of smoke filled her nose.

"Mom, what are you *doing*?" asked Penelope again. Her mother stared at her, speechless. Penelope touched her hair. Gray clumps of the bubbling gunk hung from her fingers. She felt a burning sensation in her nose, and her eyes started watering.

Wham! Suddenly, everything fell into place.

"You've been dyeing my hair all this time! It's never been gray—it was always red, and you've been covering it up all these years with that stuff. But you've been away so long that the real color's come back!" Hastily, she rubbed the paste off her head. Her mother still hadn't moved. "But why, Mom? Why?"

No movement. Not a word. Her mom appeared to be in shock. Coco jumped onto Mrs. Gardener's lap and pushed her nose into her stomach, and finally her mother whispered: "Because you're my everything. Because I don't want to lose you."

Her eyes filled with tears. She blinked, and the tears ran down her face. Penelope threw her arms around her mother.

"But Mom, you haven't lost me—it's just the opposite!

I feel like I'm *me* for the first time in my life, like I'm complete at last. There's no question of you losing me!"

But this just made her mother cry even more. Penelope was totally confused. She let go of her mother and pulled her legs up to her body so that her red hair flowed over her knees. Her heart was thumping wildly and her tongue as well . . . Why should telling her mother how totally *herself* she felt with red hair make her cry?

The moon emerged from behind a cloud, shining into the room and bathing the furniture, her mother, and Penelope in its silvery light. Another realization hit Penelope like a physical blow. Suddenly, she knew she wasn't the only one in the family to be blessed with hair like hers: She'd *inherited* this hair.

"Tell me about Dad," she said softly. Mrs. Gardener looked up, opened her mouth, and nodded silently.

7

Love at First Sight

"Your father and I met at an auction for a run-down old cottage," Penelope's mother began. "Lots of people had come to bid for it, but I noticed the handsome red-haired man in the dark overcoat straightaway. Neither of us bid enough money for the cottage, and when the auction finished, the handsome man said to me, 'Now we've saved ourselves a bit of cash, how about we go and spend some of it together?' There was such a sparkle in his eyes as he said it that I couldn't help but agree. But there wasn't really anywhere to spend our money nearby, so we went for a long walk in the countryside instead.

"Everything this red-haired man said made so much sense, everything he did was so natural and so casual that at first I didn't notice that he was different . . . that he was simply an impossibility. As we walked, he plucked berries from the bushes for me, even though it was spring. He picked young leaves, pressed them gently against his cheek, stroked them flat between his hands, and in the next moment butterflies flew out from between his fingers. He grabbed me around my waist, lifted me up, spun around, and suddenly we were sitting on the highest branch of an oak tree. He took my hand, looked at me, and said, 'We'll be happy together, you and I, and I'll be there for you for as long as I live. Would you like that? Would you like to be my wife?' I nodded, as I knew deep inside that he was the love of my life. Even though I barely knew him."

Penelope's mother paused and fiddled with the buttons on her blouse, her eyes unusually bright. She looked out the window into the moonlit night, then took a deep breath and carried on.

"The time we spent together was the happiest time of my life. Everything felt simple and easy. As I said, your father was different, so from time to time he had to go away for a few days—he needed to spend time with people of his own kind, he said. Just for a little while, so as not to get 'rusty.' When he came back from these meet-ups, he was always radiant with energy and good humor, he would seem even livelier than usual. And he'd sweep me along with his verve and his laughter. Until one day he came home with his face as white as a sheet. He just said a brief 'hello' to me, and then went straight into our bedroom. I could hear some funny noises—glasses clinking, a sort of hissing sound, and there was a banging noise from time to time too. When your father came back out, his beautiful long red hair was completely gray, like an old man's.

"'What have you done?!' I shouted. I was horrified. But he just smiled and took my hands.

"'I've disguised myself.'

"I didn't know if that was supposed to be a joke, and if it was one, I certainly wasn't laughing. He pulled me to him and said, 'I've taken the color out of my hair to make myself invisible.'

"'Umm, Leo,' I said gently, wondering if he'd lost his mind, 'I'm sorry, but you're not invisible. I can see you as clear as day. You're standing right in front of me with a blue pullover on, and gray hair.'

"'That's not what I mean,' he said softly. 'It's made me invisible to my kind. Of course, they'll still be able to see me, but they won't be able to *feel* me—they won't be able to sense that I'm one of them.'

"'What do you mean? Why are you afraid of them sensing you?'

"'Trust me, Lucia, it's better if I don't tell you too much about it. Not right now, anyway. I want to spend my life with you, only with you. You're what matters most to me . . . you're my everything. I'm just going to become an ordinary man, we'll move somewhere no one knows us, and we can lead a peaceful life.'

"So we moved here. We bought this little house and

painted it red. Once a month, Leo painted his hair with his peculiar gray paste to hide the color, and to suppress the powers that his hair gave him. It stayed gray and he stayed undiscovered. But occasionally, if he was completely sure that none of the people he was afraid of were hanging around the area, he left the paste off and kept his hair red for a few hours. 'I need to do that from time to time,' he told me. 'Otherwise I can't develop—I'll be stuck at the stage I'm at right now.' He would go off into the swamp forest to discover new things—how to make stones float, for example."

Penelope gazed at her mother, mesmerized, her eyes bright.

"And then you came along," Mom said tenderly. "I was already so happy, but Penny, when you came into our lives, I felt as though the sun would never set again. Your eyes were clear and dark and your voice was as powerful as a storm. Leo was enchanted by you too. You didn't have a single hair on your head, you were as bald as a coot, and he was bursting with curiosity about what color hair you were going to have.

"One evening, he said, 'I need to go and spend some time on my practicing tomorrow. Will you be OK if I leave you alone with our Penny all day?' That was fine by me, of course, so that night he left the ash paste off. It had been a month since he last applied it, and so the next morning his hair shone redder than the sun, and as he went out of the door, it looked like he was flying rather than walking. He nodded to me, blew me a kiss, and . . . well, that was the last time I ever saw him." Penelope's mother looked down at her sadly. "He wasn't here by the time your first hair appeared. Your first flame-red wisps of hair."

"What?!" Penelope exclaimed. She had been so captivated by the fairy tale of her parents' marriage that this abrupt ending felt unbearable. "But where did he go? He can't have just disappeared—that's impossible!"

"That's what I kept thinking at first: *But this is impossible. It's simply impossible.* But the letter he wrote me after he'd been gone for a few months didn't leave any room for misunderstanding."

"What sort of letter?"

Penelope's mother reached into her pocket and pulled out a worn piece of paper. She handed it to her daughter. "Even though I can't bear to read it, I've never felt strong enough to throw it away," she said softly.

Penelope read the letter.

Dear Lucia,

You have always known that I am different. I'm sorry, but recently in the forest, I met a lady who is the same as me. And suddenly I realized that a part of me had been missing all this time. I don't want to pretend anymore—I need to be myself again, so I think it's best if I stay away. I'll make sure Penelope is provided for.

Best wishes,

Leo Arthur

When she had finished reading, she returned the letter to her mom. "What happened then?" she asked.

Her mother had slumped in her seat, but now she straightened up. She looked at Penelope and shrugged, slipping the letter into her pocket.

"I cried for months, I prayed, I thought I would surely die. But I didn't die, because I had you to look after. You needed food and clean diapers and arms to hold you. Your laughter was balm for my broken heart. But the day your hair started to grow, I thought it was all over. It was as red as flames, and as beautiful as your father's. I was filled with fear straightaway, because I knew you might have inherited more than just his hair color. So I took the big glass of ash paste out of Leo's cupboard and painted it onto your hair. It turned as gray as stone, and I felt calmer again. Then when you were a little older, and the hearing-before-hearing started, I knew I was right—you hadn't just inherited his hair color. Penny, believe me, I didn't do it to try and stop you finding out that you had all these powers. I was just so terrified that you'd leave me, just like your father had."

Penelope took a deep breath. She felt as though she'd been holding her breath for the past half hour.

"And then?" she asked.

"And then nothing. That was that. He's gone, and I hope he stays away—I want nothing more to do with him." Her mother's voice was now hard and brisk, as if she wanted the conversation to be over.

But Penelope hadn't finished. "But what was all that with the letter?"

"How do you know about that letter? Oh, never mind, it doesn't matter now. Leo sends me money for you every month, just like he promised," her mother said, her voice full of bitterness. "The gray envelope always arrives on the seventh, and has banknotes stuffed into it—never a card or anything personal, just money. And this month he has obviously decided to play an especially funny joke and only sent five dollars. Oh, how we laughed!"

Strangely, Penelope felt uncomfortable with her mother's anger. She was angry with her father, too, of course—she couldn't believe how he'd abandoned them both—but in spite of that, she didn't like to hear her mother speaking badly of him. It felt wrong, somehow.

"And you've never written back?"

"I haven't got an address for him, and I wouldn't write to him even if I did." Her mother's voice was tight and pained. She stood up.

Penelope was insistent. "But what about the post-mark? Where are the letters stamped?"

"Somewhere called Blackslough. And now you should sleep, my darling. Let's talk about this some more in the morning, shall we? I'm tired."

"And the rain on my birthday," Penelope said as her mom turned toward the door. "The rain that isn't really wet—has that got something to do with Dad too?"

"I've no idea, Penelope. Really. Now please go to sleep!"

Penelope nodded and turned off the light, but her mind was spinning and she knew it would be ages before she fell asleep. She had a father who was alive—a father with red hair and special powers, a father who liked to laugh and who discovered new things, a father who lived in Blackslough and sent a letter every month in a gray envelope.

She needed to let it all sink in.

8

Street Acquaintances

Early morning light flooded Penelope's room. Awakened by the brightness, she jumped out of bed. *It's Mom's first day home*, she remembered as she washed her face. *I'm going to get fresh rolls from the village to celebrate!* She skipped downstairs. *And I have a father now too. A father who's alive! It's so exciting I could ride up and down the hill three times.*

She shook some cat food energetically into Coco's bowl and put some fresh water next to it, then pulled on her blue sandals and opened the front door. The world outside shone so brightly that Penelope was dazzled. She blinked and glanced down, watching a gray-and-yellow cellar spider running up the steps and into the house. Coco, who was padding downstairs, didn't notice the eight-legged visitor—she only had eyes for her overflowing food bowl.

Penelope fetched her bike from the shed and pushed it up the sand path between the fragrant herbs. She paused by the old beech tree and breathed in deeply. What a beautiful morning—so full of light, air, and birdsong. The empty road stretched uphill toward the village, threading its way through the taller green hills beyond, before disappearing into the forest way off in the distance.

Penelope hoisted her bike onto the pavement and began to pedal laboriously uphill. She hadn't got very far when she heard a loud clattering, and the next moment a tractor appeared at the top of the hill—but it wasn't just any tractor, she realized as it started to descend. It was *the* tractor—the green one that had soaked her through, the one she was nearly certain had knocked over her mother. Immediately, she rode to the side of the road and hopped off her bike. A fleeting shiver passed across the back of her neck as she caught sight of the driver, his gold-framed sunglasses flashing in the bright sunshine. *Someone like me*, she thought, all of a sudden, without really knowing what that meant. The tractor was roaring down the hill, far too fast, and it had nearly reached her . . . but something was wrong: Penelope noticed the driver was heading straight for her, even though she stood on the pavement. The engine roared, the wheels screamed—and suddenly the huge vehicle loomed over her. Penelope was frozen to the spot. She couldn't scream, she couldn't move, she couldn't jump out of the tractor's path. Her young life was already over. Finished, done. Squished by an enormous green machine, crushed under heavy twin tires. She screwed her eyes shut.

She felt an impact, a sort of jarring sensation within her. But she hadn't fallen—she was still standing. Was this how death felt? No, that was impossible—she felt exactly the same as she always did, only a little more scared. Penelope opened her eyes and blinked in disbelief: The tractor was teetering on two tires, leaning toward the opposite side of the road. It looked as though it was standing in midair, trying to decide whether to right itself or topple over onto its side. Suddenly, the road appeared to twitch, the tractor jolted, and the two hovering wheels slammed back down onto the road, shaking the ground. Penelope blinked again. What had happened? Had the road . . . moved? Abruptly, the road under the tractor started to snake downhill, like a conveyer belt.

What?!

Penelope watched as the road gathered speed. The man driving the tractor was revving the engine and turning the wheel wildly—but it wasn't working. Before long, the tractor disappeared down the hill so fast that it looked like a piece of film on fast-forward.

A little frightened, Penelope hopped back on her bike and started pedaling uphill as fast as possible, glancing occasionally over her shoulder.

Penelope didn't slow down until the tractor had been swallowed up by the forest. She stopped, dismounted, and took a deep breath, clinging on to the handlebars. *What the heck's going on here?* she wondered dazedly.

"WELL, YOU DID SAY I SHOULD HAVE TAKEN THE GUY AROUND SOME OTHER BEND LAST TIME."

Penelope spun round.

"BUT THERE WASN'T A BEND AVAILABLE, SO I THOUGHT PERHAPS AN UNEVEN SURFACE AND A BIT OF ACCELERATION MIGHT DO THE JOB INSTEAD."

A voice like soft thunder boomed all around her—but where was it coming from? From near or far, from the ground or the village, she couldn't tell. Or was it coming from inside her head?

"DON'T LOOK SO AFRAID. YOU WERE GOING SOMEWHERE, WEREN'T YOU? IF YOU STAND AROUND ON ME FOR MUCH LONGER, YOU MIGHT START TO TAKE ROOT."

Penelope gasped as her feet jumped a little way off

the ground. It felt as if someone had gently punched their soles. She looked at the ground beneath her, the paving slabs shimmering slightly in the morning light.

"Is that you?" whispered Penelope.

"WHO ELSE?" the road replied.

"But, but . . ."

"'BUT, BUT' NOTHING," rumbled the road, and suddenly, Penelope and her bicycle were zooming forward of their own accord, as though the bike were on a conveyor belt. Penelope found herself zipping from the paving slabs onto the asphalt surface of the road, which whizzed under the wheels of her bike, carrying her into the village. But when she tried to stop at the baker's, she lost her balance and fell face-first onto the road. A dull rumbling noise came from the road.

Quickly, Penelope scrambled to her feet, dusted herself off, and nodded to the lady who was just coming out of the baker's, as if nothing untoward had happened. She hurried into the shop to buy the rolls. When she emerged again, she looked all around her before hesitantly placing a foot on the gray road.

"YOU DON'T NEED TO BE SO TIMID," the thunderous voice intoned. "I'M USED TO PEOPLE TRAMPLING ON ME, DRIVING ON ME, ROLLING ON ME, DRILLING ON ME—YOU NAME IT. TO ME, YOUR FEET FEEL A BIT LIKE A SOOTHING MASSAGE."

Penelope smiled shyly. "OK." Nevertheless, she swung herself onto her bike more carefully than usual, and pedaled smoothly downhill. She was back at the beech tree in no time at all.

"Thank you," she whispered as she left the road and stepped onto the sand track. "Thank you for the lift. And—for what you did with the tractor."

"NO PROBLEM. SO, THEN, UNTIL TOMORROW, WHEN YOU GO TO SCHOOL. I THINK I'LL PROBABLY STILL BE HERE THEN." The rumbling voice shook a little. Was the road laughing? "ALTHOUGH I SUPPOSE IT'S ALWAYS POSSIBLE THAT I MIGHT HAVE BEEN DIVERTED."

"Um . . . OK." Penelope was glad she was standing on the sand track, as the paving slabs in front of her were shaking with amusement.

9

Making Friends with the Road

The breakfast table was already laid as Penelope walked into the dragon house, and as she unwrapped her package from the baker, the bread rolls smelled delicious. Her mother walked through the kitchen, humming, and planted a kiss on Penelope's forehead. She smiled. She wished she could tell her mother about the strange experience on the road, but Granny Elizabeth was already at the table, and Penelope didn't want to say anything while she was there.

After breakfast, Mrs. Gardener suggested a walk. *Hopefully Granny will stay at home*, thought Penelope, but today of all days, apparently, G.E. absolutely *had* to have some exercise.

They set off along the narrow path through the swamp forest, emerging into the spring-wet meadows. The sun blazed high in the sky, and the air was filled with the buzzing of flies and bumblebees. As Penelope tramped between her mother and G.E., she realized she was going to have to wait before she could talk to her mother in private.

After a while, they came to the stone circle, a ring of gray and reddish boulders that someone had arranged in the middle of the meadow. Penelope had often wondered how they'd got there, but nobody seemed to know anything about them. Except that today, all of a sudden, it seemed that her mother *did* know something, after all.

"Your father put these rocks here," she admitted quietly as they drew to a halt in the center of the circle. "He transported them here himself. Don't ask me how... all he'd tell me was that he'd asked for the stones, and they'd appeared."

"Well, he left us a nice picnic spot, I'll give him that,"

muttered Granny Elizabeth, leaning against one of the boulders.

Penelope climbed up onto the smallest rock and looked at her mother, who was unfolding a blanket for their picnic. She felt so much closer to her now, she realized. They'd always gotten along, but because Mrs. Gardener had never talked about Penelope's father, there had always been a hole in Penelope's heart. This hole had made her feel distant from her mother at times. But now the emptiness was starting to fill up with stories about her father. Penelope loved the feeling that her heart was growing full, and she loved her father too. Or, at least, she loved one of her fathers.

Because she felt as though she had two fathers now: the one who had lived with her mother, who had laughed a lot and made such wonderful things happen . . . and the other father: the one who'd simply disappeared, who'd left them both for another woman. Penelope didn't love the second father at all. She was angry with him, and whenever she dwelled on him, her thoughts grew narrow and gloomy.

“Penelope? Why don’t you sit down?” Her mom smiled up at her from the blanket she’d laid out on the grass. G.E. was already tucking into a sandwich.

As she joined the picnic, Penelope glared at the stone circle in sudden fury. One day, she would meet that second father and tell him exactly what she thought of him.

They carried on walking into the late afternoon, following a narrow path that ran alongside a blackthorn hedge and then petered out across an uncultivated field. They continued across the field, their route starting to curve back toward home, and soon reached a small country lane that separated the field from a meadow. As the three of them crossed the lane, a great rattling and thundering rose up from the ground.

“BY THE WAY, IT’S BETTER IF YOU DON’T TELL ANYONE ELSE ABOUT ME.”

Penelope jumped in fright, recognizing the booming voice of the road. “What? Oh . . . well, OK,” she muttered.

"'Well, OK' what?" Mrs. Gardener turned to her daughter, confused. "Did you hear something just then?"

"Didn't *you* hear anything?"

"No. Should we have?" asked Granny Elizabeth and her mother at the same time.

Penelope shook her head quickly. "No, no." She hurriedly suggested a race, desperate for a distraction. "Whoever gets to the birch tree first is the winner!" Penelope started running across the meadow.

Her mother hesitated briefly, but then ran after her, and even Granny Elizabeth started to jog, though rather more slowly.

"Even if you can hear and see things we can't," Penelope's mother called after her, "there's one thing we can see that you can't . . . and that's your blazing red hair trailing out behind you like fire!" Her mother laughed as she gained on Penelope. Penelope laughed too. And—to Penelope's surprise—Granny Elizabeth laughed as well.

But the next moment, her grandmother's laughter died, replaced by a strangled "Aaaahhhhhhhh!"

Penelope stopped and turned. Granny Elizabeth had stopped and was pulling her right foot upward.

"What is it?" Mrs. Gardener asked, running back to her.

"Twisted my ankle," Granny Elizabeth groaned. "Heavens above, it hurts." Her face suddenly turned as translucent as the paper-like bark of the birch. "Aah-aah-aah! I need to sit down." She dropped onto the grass, pearls of sweat on her forehead.

"Let's have a look." Mrs. Gardener started to remove her mother's boot, but when she pulled, Granny Elizabeth screamed in pain. The sweat ran down her face in small streams.

"I think I—" she murmured, then slumped backward onto the grass. She blinked briefly, but was silent.

"What's the matter?" Penelope dropped to her knees beside her mother. She shook her grandmother's shoulder and tapped her cheek lightly. But Granny Elizabeth lay there in the grass with her eyes closed, unmoving.

"She's fainted. You know she can't cope very well with pain. That was probably a bit too much for her just now. Oh, and there's no phone reception out here! Stay with her—I'm going to run home and get help." Before Penelope could answer her mother, she'd already hurried off.

Penelope took Granny Elizabeth's hand and stroked it. "Can you hear me?" she murmured. But apparently Granny couldn't. And so Penelope waited for her mother to fetch help, watching particles of light filter down from the branches to the grass and dance in the evening sun. She looked across the wide fields, listening to the rustling of the grass. Clouds were gathering overhead.

Suddenly, the voice of the road resounded in her ear: "IT'LL BE LONG PAST DARK BY THE TIME HELP ARRIVES, AND THERE'S A THUNDERSTORM BREWING. PUT THE LADY ONTO ME, AND I'LL TAKE IT FROM THERE."

"Really?" Penelope stood up, grasping G.E. under the arms. She pulled and tugged, but her grandmother was heavier than she'd thought. She managed to move her about an inch, but they were still a hundred yards or more from the little lane.

"YOU NEED TO MAKE MORE EFFORT," boomed the road. "I CAN ONLY BEND WHEN IT RAINS—THE SUN MAKES ME AS STIFF AS A DRY WORM—OTHERWISE I'D HELP YOU."

Penelope tried to roll Granny Elizabeth, but it wasn't easy. "I'm doing my best," she panted.

"NO, YOU'RE NOT. WHAT YOU'RE DOING IS JUST A WASTE OF ENERGY. YOU'VE GOT TOO MUCH CABBAGE IN YOUR HEAD, OTHERWISE YOU'D BE DOING WHAT YOU'RE REALLY CAPABLE OF."

Penelope couldn't believe her ears. Here she was, dragging and pushing and rolling for all she was worth, and this bumpy little road had the nerve to speak to her in that tone! And what did that even mean—"cabbage in her head" and "doing what she was really capable of"?

"STAND FIRM AND GROW STRONG."

Penelope didn't know what it meant by "stand firm,"

and she certainly didn't know how to "grow strong." But some instinct told her to try. She stood, calmly, silently, and closed her eyes.

After a few moments, her feet began to tingle, and then to twitch. Penelope had the sense they were rooting themselves in the ground somehow. And then, with a gasp, she felt a great power beginning to flow through her, rising up from the ground. Her whole body tingled now. She was drawing strength from the ground! *Good*, thought Penelope, *that's good. I really am feeling stronger.* She tried to breathe slowly and evenly, but it was difficult when some kind of electrical impulse was hissing through her body.

Oh! She felt herself grow airy all of a sudden, as light and permeable as the wind. Her body gave a jerk, and she looked down.

"Stop! Stop! Stop! Stop! Stop! Sto-o-o-p!"

This was all going very wrong. She didn't want to be light, she wanted to be strong . . . but . . . her feet! Her feet, in their blue sandals . . . they were floating in the air!

10

Upward and Forward

Well, "in the air" was perhaps a slight exaggeration: Her sandals were a quarter of an inch above the ground. And then it was half an inch, and then an inch. Penelope had no idea what to do. Now she was two inches above the ground, now four. Blades of grass waved beneath her feet, the trees rustled above her, and her heart was hammering in her chest. Higher and higher she rose. Oh, no! Now she was already a foot and a half in the air. If this carried on, she might end up having to send her mother a postcard: *Sorry, had to fly. Greetings from the moon, Penelope.*

But she had to admit, there was something very nice about floating—she could let herself be carried along, rocking gently on the current of the wind, and look down at the world from up above. She could . . .

A chain of geese flew over, silhouetted against the pinkening sky like a moving letter V. The birds' throaty, squealing cries echoed down to Penelope, dragging her back to reality. Instinctively, she reached into her hair with both hands, feeling her wild tangle of curls fizzing with power, and pulled down on it hard. Immediately she jolted to a stop. She lurched, and the strange electrical impulse hissed through her body again. She hung there, three feet above the ground now, clutching her hair tightly and feeling relieved. She cleared her throat.

"What now?" she wondered aloud.

"BE CALM," the road rumbled. "FINISH WHAT YOU HAVE BEGUN. FOCUS YOUR MIND AND RELEASE THE LIGHTNESS YOU'VE COLLECTED. LET IT FLOAT DOWN TO YOUR GRANDMOTHER."

Penelope looked at Granny Elizabeth. She looked at

her plump stomach and her wrinkled hands, and as she did so, her own body became heavier and slowly began to sink. As her sandals touched the grass, Granny Elizabeth rose slightly into the air. It was barely visible, but her grandmother's bulky body was floating a few millimeters above the ground.

Cautiously, Penelope let go of her hair and waited for the road's next instruction.

"NOW FOR THE DIFFICULT PART," boomed the road. "NOW YOU DO NOTHING. ALL YOU HAVE TO DO IS CONCENTRATE ON DIRECTION. THE GOOD LADY NEEDS TO BE PLACED ONTO ME, NOT HANGING AROUND IN THE AIR. CONCENTRATE AND WAIT. THAT'S ALL. YOU MUSTN'T DISTURB THE PROCESS OR GET IMPATIENT."

Penelope took a deep breath and let her thoughts travel the distance between herself and the road. The sun was setting behind the trees, and the shadow of the birch tree was beginning to fade when, all of a sudden—*whoosh!* Like a dry autumn leaf blown by the wind, Granny Elizabeth slid across the meadow all by herself. She wobbled a little, then slid farther along, until—*whoomp*—she had landed on the road.

Penelope exhaled heavily, then started to run over to where her grandmother lay.

"PERFECT POSITIONING." The words rumbled around her. "NOW, TAKE HER HAND AND WALK ALONG BESIDE HER."

Penelope obeyed, stumbling along on the grass beside the sliding road, clutching her grandmother's hand. She quickly felt tired. "Can't I ride on you as well?"

The ground beneath her shook a little. "I CAN ONLY DO THIS FOR ONE PERSON AT A TIME IN EACH DIRECTION—I'M A ROAD, NOT A SUPERMARKET CHECKOUT. AND YOU'RE NOT A PACKET OF COOKIES, ARE YOU?"

"All right, keep your hair on," muttered Penelope. She started to jog, as the road set quite a challenging pace.

They were more than halfway home, when—*ka-wumm!*—Penelope's hand was dragged from Granny Elizabeth's and she fell hard onto the paving slabs.

"What was that about, road?!" She rubbed her knee. "One minute we're breaking the speed limit, and the next we're making an emergency stop?"

"THERE'S A REASON—YOU'LL SOON SEE." The pavement vibrated as it spoke.

A moment later, a car's headlights appeared over the hill. Penelope realized how dark it had grown, and glanced up at the sky—mountains of dark clouds hid the sun. At the sound of the car's engine, Granny Elizabeth opened her eyes, gazed around her in astonishment, and muttered something that sounded like, "Can't remember a thing." She tried to stand up.

Penelope scrambled quickly to her feet and held out her arm for Granny Elizabeth to lean on. "Can you manage?"

"How should I know?" she said irritably.

The car pulled up, and Mom stepped out of the passenger seat. A man Penelope recognized from the neighborhood got out of the driver's side. The expression on Mrs. Gardener's face changed in a moment from very relieved to utterly confused.

The neighbor hurried to help Granny Elizabeth into the car. "How did you do that?" whispered Mrs. Gardener to Penelope.

"I'll tell you later," whispered Penelope. She was still trying to make sense of it herself.

As they clambered into the back of the car, the first bolt of lightning flashed against the dark sky, closely followed by an echoing crack of thunder. All of a sudden, the rain hammered down on the surrounding meadows. Penelope couldn't even see any raindrops in the car's headlights: The rain was a flat wall of water. Now she was more than grateful that the road had hurried her along—if she'd been out in this weather, she'd have been soaked through to the bone in seconds. Their neighbor had to drive very slowly because it was coming down so hard, and from time to time he even stopped altogether.

"Controlled driving is essential in these conditions," he expounded. "It's vital not to overestimate one's own capabilities, or the vehicle's." He patted the steering wheel gently. "Though, of course, I do like to get some speed up from time to time too. It's important to really open the engine up regularly. I'll take you on a motorway tour sometime if you like," he said to Penelope's mother. "Then you can see what a good bit of equipment I've got under this hood." On and on he went, and he didn't appear to notice when the rain had stopped as suddenly as it had started. He continued driving at an agonizing crawl.

Penelope rolled her eyes, and Mrs. Gardener asked tentatively if perhaps they could get moving again.

"Of course, but one must always bear in mind that the road is very unpredictable in wet weather conditions."

Penelope had to smile at that. *And in sunny conditions too*, she thought affectionately.

11

News from Pete

That night Penelope dreamt about floating. She was drifting weightlessly over the dragon house, and she couldn't find a way to come down, no matter how hard she pulled on her hair. Suddenly, a red-haired man with laughing eyes popped his head out of the chimney and called out, "The hair pulling is just for beginners anyway. There's a completely different method of accomplishing that kind of thing." But he didn't say what the method was, and a moment later, Penelope woke up.

The dream was already fading, and soon she

couldn't remember anything about it; all that remained was the strange floaty feeling it had left behind. She wished she had someone to talk to about all the bizarre things that had taken place over the past few days, someone who could lend her a little support. There was the road, of course, but the road was just that: a road, not a person—besides which, the road itself was one of the bizarre things.

"Penny! Breakfast's ready!" Her mother sounded cheerful, at least.

Penelope came downstairs to find a huge tower of pancakes on her plate and all sorts of toppings scattered across the kitchen table. Immediately, she forgot all about her strange floaty feeling and her wish for support. Instead, she sat down and started eating.

Pancakes with sugar and lemon. Pancakes with applesauce. Pancakes with maple syrup. Pancakes with raspberry jam. *Mmm!* Her mom's pancakes were simply the best—once you started, it was impossible to stop eating them! But after the eighth pancake, Penelope's stomach started to ache. And after the ninth, she felt as round as a ball, and so heavy and full that she couldn't imagine going to school by any stretch of the imagination. But her mother could imagine it perfectly well, so she pressed Penelope's schoolbag into her hand, planted a kiss on her cheek, and shooed her out of the house.

Penelope plodded heavily along, pushing her bike over the bumpy track and resolving never to eat again. *The others will think I've turned into a beach ball,* she thought as she huffed and puffed her way up the track. *But perhaps my luck will be in—if I can get myself to the beech tree, the road might give me a lift up the hill.*

"Morning," she called out when she got there, lifting her bike onto the pavement. The road wound its way sluggishly between the hills, as though it was asleep. Penelope cleared her throat and waited. But the ground didn't shake, and no thunderous voice could be heard. Everything remained silent and peaceful.

"Don't you do mornings, then?"

No reply. Penelope took that to mean no. She sighed, and pedaled laboriously up to the bus stop under her own steam.

Everyone gathered around Penelope on the school bus, and later in the classroom, a crowd formed around her again, but it wasn't due to Penelope's transformation into a beach ball.

"Cool dye job!"

"That hair makes you shine like the sun!"

"Wow, wow, wow!"

Of course—her hair! Penelope had grown so used to it over the weekend that she had completely forgotten that the others hadn't seen her blazing red tangle of hair. Kids from every class thronged around her; even some of the seventh graders had come to have a look.

"How come you've never done that before? It looks super cool!" her deskmate Anna-Lea asked, tugging gently on a strand of Penelope's hair.

Mr. Potts waved his hands and tried in vain to call the rabble to order, but no one paid him any attention. Finally, he had to resort to striking the big gong that he always used when his lessons needed a bit of crowd control.

"Out, out, everyone, please!" he scolded them, though his voice was friendly. "You all have lessons to go to, even if our dear Miss Gardener is looking extra elegant and vibrant today. That hair tops even Tom's and Pete's golden locks."

But Pete seemed to have more pressing issues than hair color on his mind. At break time, he pulled Penelope abruptly to one side. "Is Coco your cat?" he asked, with an uncertain look on his face.

"Yes . . . why do you ask?"

Pete didn't reply, but asked further: "And do you know what Blackslough is?"

Penelope gasped—it was where her father lived, of course, but she hadn't told anyone about that. "What are you talking about?" she snapped, her eyes flashing, then immediately regretted her tone when she saw the nervous expression on Pete's face.

"I don't know anything," he stammered. "I—I—I thought perhaps *you* might know."

Penelope softened her tone. "Oh, did you really? And why would you think that?"

"Because . . . because . . ." Pete's voice died away. It was only when Penelope put a reassuring hand on his arm that he grew a little calmer. "Because I heard someone saying: 'Bring Coco to Blackslough, please, bring Coco to Blackslough.'"

Penelope felt the color drain from her face. Was someone trying to kidnap her cat? "Who said that to you?"

"That's just it—no one said it to me. I just heard these voices in my head, you know? I was kicking the ball around up on the soccer field on my own. I couldn't see a single person, but all of a sudden there was the first voice—it was sort of soft and warm—and it said that about Coco."

Penelope took a step backward and looked Pete up and down. She took in his blue sneakers, one lace blue and the other one orange, his skinny legs in worn jeans, his baggy black sweater, and his light blond hair. Was it possible? Was he, too, perhaps . . . ?

"Can you do it too? The hearing-before-hearing thing?"

"The what?" Pete raised his eyebrows.

"Well, I mean . . . do you ever know what your mom's going to say before she speaks to you?"

"Oh, yeah. Every time." Pete grinned. "Either she says, 'Tidy your room,' or she says, 'Tidy your room this minute.'"

Penelope shook her head. "That's not what I mean. I mean . . . do you ever hear your mom or dad say something, as if they were actually speaking when they aren't?"

"Penny, please, I can't do anything like that. I'd probably have forgotten about this altogether, if it was just the first voice, but then I heard another voice, and that one said your name—Gardener, I mean—so I thought I'd better ask you about it." He shifted uneasily from one foot to the other. "That voice, I mean the second one, it wasn't friendly—there was something cold and slippery about it. It called out, 'Is that bit of blue string your new plaything, then, Gardener?' Then everything went quiet again. I waited for ages, and after a while, I started to wonder if I'd imagined it all. So I shoved it to the back of my mind and carried on playing. But then, when I saw you this morning, I thought perhaps I should tell you . . . perhaps you'd know if it means anything."

Penelope was lost for words. Nothing Pete had told her made any sense. Her tongue began to click softly, and her knees felt shaky. But then she drew herself upright. *I'm Penelope Gardener*, she thought, *and I'm going to find out what's going on with this strange voice.*

"Thanks for telling me about it," she said to Pete. "I think it could be important, and if I can work out what's going on, I'll tell you. But it's break time now. C'mon, let's go and find the others."

12

A Full Head

Doing homework when your mind is on something else can be quite time-consuming. That afternoon, Penelope sat for the better part of three hours, supposedly working on her English essay, and only managed to write two sentences. Not very impressive, especially as neither sentence had anything whatsoever to do with the essay topic. The first sentence was written in large letters on the sheet of lined paper in front of Penelope:

BRING COCO TO BLACKSLOUGH

And, farther down the page in slightly smaller letters:

IS THAT BIT OF BLUE STRING
YOUR NEW PLAYTHING?

Penelope had written the sentences down because she hoped it'd help her to understand them, and stop them turning over and over in her head. It wasn't really working. She went back over what she did know: For starters, Pete couldn't do the hearing-before-hearing thing, that much was obvious. His hair wasn't red, and besides, Penelope always felt completely normal when she was around him, whereas her father had said that people like them could sense each other's presence. But why had Pete heard what he'd heard? And who had said it to him?

"Holy swamp cow! This isn't getting me anywhere." Penelope stood up abruptly and set off outside to clear her head. The fresh air in her face felt good, and blew away her tiredness.

Penelope decided to wander to the stone circle to try out the floating. It started well, though she couldn't float any higher than the smallest rocks, barely three feet above the ground. It was as though the power drained away if she went above a certain height, or as if there was something pressing down on her from above and stopping her from getting any higher. *Maybe I just need more practice*, she thought, lowering herself back down to earth. She decided she'd practice every day from then on. And she'd stick a tape measure to her bedroom wall to keep a record of her progress.

As she set off down the road home, she started thinking about her mother and father, and even G.E., and what sort of things each of them had passed on to her. Although she didn't know her father, he'd given her something extraordinary.

"YES INDEED, FAMILY IS NOT TO BE UNDERESTIMATED," the road boomed all of a sudden. Penelope almost fell off her bike in fright, but then she laughed.

"That's right! You and your family, dear road, are really not to be underestimated."

The road rumbled grumpily and boomed something indistinct. It sounded a bit like "I HAVE NO FAMILY. I'M ALONE."

Penelope was a little unsure how to respond to that. She wondered if she was supposed to comfort the road over its solitude. "But you're not alone," she tried. "There are loads of other roads. And there are new ones being built all the time, and . . ."

"NONSENSE! THERE ARE NO OTHER ROADS. THAT'S ALL ME!"

Penelope frowned in puzzlement.

"HAVE YOU EVER SEEN A ROAD THAT JUST STARTS AND FINISHES IN THE MIDDLE OF NOWHERE?" asked the road. "EVERY ROAD LEADS TO ANOTHER ROAD," it went on, not waiting for a reply. "EVERY ROAD IS CONNECTED TO THE NEXT, EVERYONE IS TOGETHER WITH EVERYONE, EVERYTHING IS UNITED."

Penelope pedaled harder. "Well, yeah, but . . ."

"THERE ARE NO OTHERS! I AM ALL!" the voice of

the road boomed, from farther away this time. Then it fell silent.

"OK, OK, well, I'm not all, I'm just Penelope Gardener. And I think my head will burst if I try to stuff any more thoughts into it today."

13

Practice, Practice, Practice

A few weeks passed, and the weather grew gradually hotter as spring turned to summer. Often, the sun burned so relentlessly by eight o'clock in the morning that Penelope took the cool swamp forest path, even though that meant she couldn't talk to the road. The road wasn't often up for conversation at that hour anyway—it was fond of claiming it had spent all night twisting and turning, and hadn't slept a wink.

When the weather was this hot, most of the local children met up after school by a small lake in the forest. They held swimming contests, dared each other to dive off tree stumps, or rode through the water on slippery tree trunks. When they'd worn themselves out, they would lie in the shade of the large pine trees, drinking lemonade or Coke, or eating ice cream.

But this summer, Penelope didn't join the fun. It wasn't because she didn't like swimming—on the contrary, she'd hardly been out of the water the previous summer—but this year she'd been seized by ambition. Penelope's school finished at lunchtime, and she'd come home from school, eat with Granny Elizabeth and her mother, and retreat to her room, supposedly for homework. Her mother would watch her wordlessly: She knew Penelope wasn't doing her homework, but she didn't say anything. She'd been Leo Gardener's wife for long enough to know that time and space were the only things she could give her daughter to help her come to terms with all the new things she'd discovered.

Penelope had taken a tape measure up to her room. It was stuck to the wall close to the door, and was studded with red marker pins.

"Holy swamp cow! Only thirty-seven inches—again!"

She floated back down to the ground and stamped her foot so hard on the floor that the picture she and Anna-Lea had painted in art class fell off the wall and onto the bed. A startled Coco crept out from under the duvet and glared at Penelope indignantly.

"If you'd been practicing floating for weeks on end and still weren't getting any better at it, you'd stamp your foot too!" Penelope hissed at the cat. She closed her eyes again. *Wumm*—she rooted herself in the ground, felt her feet tingling and twitching, the electric power flowing through her body, and then she grew light as a feather and lifted off. She could do it in only two seconds now; she'd mastered the quick start, but she had yet to master the art of gaining height. She'd float three feet in the air, or perhaps even three feet and a bit, as she had yesterday, but that was it. She didn't even need to pull her hair in order to stop—that happened on its own once she'd reached a certain height. She never managed to float higher, whether she tried it in her room, or in the forest, or in the meadow. It didn't make any difference whether she tried it in the morning, afternoon, or evening, whether it was a full moon or new moon, whether she was tired or wide awake, whether she'd had a little or a lot to eat, whether . . .

"What am I doing wrong?" Her tongue clicked. "I must be doing *something* wrong." Was it the heat, perhaps? Or maybe people of her kind could only get up to a certain height? Yes, maybe no one could get any higher than the treetops. Maybe it was just a dream that it was possible to sail along the clouds like a swallow on the breeze.

Again Penelope wished she had someone to advise her, someone who knew how this floating thing worked, just someone she could *talk* to about all this. She'd asked the road about the height problem, but it had just thundered: "DO I LOOK LIKE SOME SORT OF EXPERT? YOU'LL JUST HAVE TO WORK IT OUT FOR YOURSELF!" And that seemed to be all it had to say on the matter.

Luckily, Penelope *had* worked something out—the "forward" part of floating, the way she'd moved Granny Elizabeth to the road, was actually quite simple. She'd learned to rise up into the air in front of the tape measure and then glide over to her desk by taking small, quick steps in the air. But she didn't much like it: Running in the air was strangely much more tiring than running on the ground.

Maybe I should just ask Mom. The thought occurred to her suddenly. *Dad might have talked to her from time to time about the things he did . . .*

There was a knock on the door of her room.

"Come in." Penelope landed on the ground again hastily, and Tom and Pete marched in.

"Are you going to come swimming with us today for once?" shouted Tom.

"Too much schoolwork's bad for your brain, you know. It's a scientific fact!" hollered Pete.

And the two of them grinned.

14

Floating with Tom and Pete

Penelope was happy to see the boys. And because it was also possible that failed attempts at flying were just as bad for the brain as homework (even if that *wasn't* a scientific fact), she accepted their invitation to go swimming. She could always ask her mother about the floating afterward.

Soon the three of them were floating on their backs in the lake, letting the water carry them along. In the blazing heat, it was almost as warm as bathwater.

"Why don't they give us time off school when it's

this hot?" Tom wondered aloud. "I really think they should."

"Yes, they should," agreed Pete. "Well, we could always suggest it. And if that goes well, they might keep it going through autumn, till the Christmas holidays or thereabouts." He smiled up thoughtfully at the sky. "We could start the new year with a break—till around Easter, maybe, or perhaps a bit longer. Then we'd go to school for two weeks so we wouldn't miss the class trip. Or the summer festival. Or field day."

Penelope smiled. It was lovely to lie here in the warm water with the two of them, imagining a life where summer vacation went on forever. She'd been so caught up in practicing floating in the air, she'd completely forgotten that a different kind of floating was also possible, and how good it felt. At any rate, it had been a long time since she'd felt as light and free as she did right now.

Afterward, they lay on the grass in the shade, and Tom opened his wonderful cooler, which was full of ice cream. "If only we could do this all summer," said Penelope longingly, "just lie here eating ice cream."

"Well, we could," said Pete. "I'm here for the whole break, at any rate—we're not going away this year."

"What? Why not?" Tom looked at his friend in astonishment. "You're normally away for most of it. First you always go on your sailing trip; then you fly off to your island villa," he said wistfully.

"Nah. Dad's sold the boat, and the island house as well. He says things have suddenly started going really badly at his business, and that he needs to cut back on his own luxuries before he has to start letting staff go."

"That sounds a bit rubbish for your dad. Great for us, though—that means we get to hang out with you for the whole summer," said Tom. He grabbed another ice cream from the cooler for each of them.

After the ice cream they went back into the water. And after the water, they had some more ice cream. Water, ice cream, water, ice cream, lemonade, water. And then Penelope realized she was dying to go to the bathroom. She walked a little way into the forest, but as she was about to squat down, a young couple came wandering through the trees, arm in arm. They stopped right in front of Penelope and turned to each other.

Penelope could have quite safely gone ahead and done what she needed to without either of them noticing, as they only had eyes for each other. But somehow it didn't seem right to pee near a kissing couple. She walked away, feeling really desperate now. Over there, behind the elderberry bush, perhaps . . . but she could see that another pair of lovebirds had beaten her to it. Holy swamp cow, what was this—Lovers' Lane? She hurried on, but her path was barred by a patch of stinging nettles.

"If I could just get over this patch . . . there's no one behind me now, and I'd finally be able to go in peace. Ohhhh, I can't stand this anymore . . ." She glanced back at the lovebirds, but they were still busy kissing. The coast was clear.

She closed her eyes, rooted herself, and started to float, the electric feeling tingling over her body. When she was higher than the stinging nettles, she began to make small steps in the air. But what was this? She was flying upward too! She wasn't doing anything different, and yet she was climbing higher. Could this really be happening? She was flying forward and upward! Forward and UPWARD! She nearly whooped with joy, but was afraid the lovebirds might glance up and spot her flying through the trees.

Woo-hoo! She'd done it! Finally she could do it! She zoomed on in delight, but suddenly—*krawumm*—she slammed into a huge, thick pine branch that had suddenly appeared in her path, as if out of nowhere, her body somersaulting clumsily over it. The branch dug itself into her shoulder, scratched her leg, and slammed against her chin, its needles lashing her face. Penelope slipped and grabbed at a twig to steady herself, but it broke and she almost fell—the tingling electric feeling had totally disappeared from her body and Penelope knew she wouldn't float. She managed to grab on to the tree just in time, clasping her legs around the trunk. Her back hurt, her head hurt. A small whimper escaped her as she clung to the rough bark.

15

Granny Elizabeth's Secret

Tom and Pete were astounded when a bashed and tattered girl suddenly plopped onto the blanket beside them.

"Penny, is that you?" asked Tom. "How the heck can someone's hair end up looking like they'd stuck their finger in a light socket, just by going for a pee? And why's half your face in shreds?"

"Button it, Tom. Can't you see she's bleeding?" Pete opened the cooler and took out the ice packs. "Here, Penelope, put these on your legs—they look like you fell into a bed of stinging nettles."

Penelope looked at him gratefully. "Next time I'll just go in the water. The forest is really a little bit dangerous." Tom and Pete were glad to see her smiling again.

"What happened back there?" asked Tom, but Penelope just looked down, played with her toes, and didn't answer.

"Earth to Penelope! I'm talking to you—what's so dangerous about our forest?"

"The pine trees," said Penelope.

"The pine trees?" Pete echoed. "I don't get it—since when have trees been dangerous?"

"Since all of a sudden they've decided to put branches right where I'm trying to get past," snapped Penelope.

Tom smirked. "You might want to give them a bit more of a wide berth, then."

"Thanks, I'll try to remember that next time. Shall we have one last splash around before we have to get back?" Penelope jumped up, raced down to the bank—"Last one in is a loser!"—and rushed into the water. Of course, neither Tom nor Pete wanted to be a loser, so they shot off, racing along neck and neck behind Penelope, trying to catch up with her tangle of red hair.

The water was warm, but it still felt good to let it run over her scratched face, although the mosquitoes and horseflies now buzzing over the water's surface were a little irritating. "I'm covered in enough bumps for one day—you can save your stings for some other time," she hissed at them, diving in quickly so she wouldn't lose her lead over the boys. They cannon balled into the water side by side, arguing over who was last. But Penelope couldn't concentrate on the argument: A question was filling her head.

Why? she kept thinking. *Why did I just start flying properly all of a sudden? What did I do differently?*

It would never have occurred to Penelope that Granny Elizabeth could help her answer that question.

When she got home that evening and G.E. saw her bruised face, the first thing she said was, "Where on earth have you been? At a boxing match?"

Penelope ignored the question. "Has Mom gone to work already?"

"Yes, it's Baroque Week. They play two concerts per evening, remember?"

Penelope sighed and drank some water straight from the tap.

"Perhaps some ointment would help these cuts to heal a little faster," murmured Granny Elizabeth suddenly.

"What sort of ointment?"

"Oh, just a healing ointment, from an old recipe. Shall I go and get it?"

Penelope nodded, and her granny went up to her room. It wasn't long before she came back down, but she wasn't carrying any ointment.

"I'm sorry, it looks like we've run out." G.E. sat back down at the kitchen table and poured a glass of milk. She made as if to drink it, but then put the glass down and looked at Penelope piercingly. "But there may be something else we could try."

"What else?" asked Penelope.

"Oh . . ." Granny Elizabeth got up and stood behind her chair, leaning against the back and running her fingernails over the pale wood, as if she was looking for fingerholds in the small notches. Then she turned and went over to the sink, turned the tap on, and began to polish the immaculately clean basin.

"Granny?"

Anyone would think there were layers of dirt on the sink, the way her grandmother was scrubbing.

"Granny?"

Now she seemed to have just discovered that the kitchen had a stove in it. She walked up to it, looking fascinated, and switched it on, then switched it off again two seconds later.

"Granny!"

G.E. turned around. "What is it?"

Penelope frowned. "Granny, what's going on? Why are you drifting round the kitchen acting all weird? *What* else could we try?"

G.E. sighed. "All right. All right, I'm going to have to tell you—there's no way around it. But not a word to your mother."

What was all this drama about? Penelope felt like rolling her eyes, but she was too curious by now, so instead she nodded quickly.

Granny Elizabeth went upstairs again without a word, and this time it was a long while before she returned to the kitchen.

When she did, she laid a slim, odd-looking book on the table. The book had a shimmering cover depicting strange coins and ornaments, and Penelope was immediately drawn to it, even though normally she wasn't much of a reader. Her fingers reached out toward it as if of their own accord, but her grandmother laid a hand on it and muttered, "I don't understand all this hocus-pocus talk, of course, but . . ."

"What kind of book is it?" Penelope was curious now.

Granny Elizabeth cleared her throat.

"After your father left, your mother either gave away or burned almost everything he owned. The only things she kept were the ash paste he'd used to dye his hair, the little black-and-white photo you've seen . . . and our old Coco, of course. But I secretly kept hold of his wonderful healing ointment. Lucia never knew a thing about it. As long as I've used it, my calluses have given me no trouble whatsoever. The same goes for warts, mosquito bites, or if I cut my finger." Granny Elizabeth chuckled.

Penelope waited patiently, hoping G.E. would say something about the book, but she didn't. She did seem to be incredibly excited, though.

"Granny, what's that got to do with the book?"

"What? Oh, yes. I took that too. It interested me because of the coins on the cover, of course, but I've never been able to understand what's inside. I can't make head or tail of it—it's certainly not about coins, at any rate. But maybe you'll be able to understand it, now that you—how can I put this?—well, now that you're one of *them* too."

One of them *too?* Penelope opened her mouth, but Granny Elizabeth was speaking again. "I mean, you might be able to understand what it says, now that Lucia isn't dyeing your hair anymore. It's possible. And if you can, and if there's an ointment recipe in there somewhere, maybe you could cook up some more healing ointment for me . . . er, I mean, for both of us? That would be wonderful, wouldn't it?" At last, she pushed the book across the table toward Penelope. "But not a word to your mother, remember?"

Penelope opened her mouth, but didn't know what to say. Her granny really was a sly old fox! She'd pinched Penelope's father's book and hidden it, she'd never told Mom, and now she wanted Penelope to use it to concoct some sort of ointment for her in secret!

Penelope must have sat there for a long time, speechless, because Granny Elizabeth suddenly pulled the book away again, looking annoyed. "Oh, well, never mind. It was just an idea."

That woke Penelope from her trance. What? Oh, no, she simply had to have this book! Quick as a flash she jumped up and grabbed the book out of G.E.'s hands, exclaiming, “But yes, Granny, I think it’s a really great idea! I’ll have a look through it and see if I can figure it out. And I won’t tell Mom.” Not waiting for a reply, she darted upstairs and into her room, clutching her booty tightly to her chest.

16

Alpha Regius

Penelope locked her bedroom door and leaned against it. She waited, her heart pounding. When she was quite sure she couldn't hear Granny Elizabeth in pursuit, she closed the window and sat down on her bed with the book. The wonderful book. The wonderful book that had belonged to her father.

Trembling a little, she spread her hands over the shimmering cover. The leather binding felt very soft and inviting, and strangely familiar somehow. There was no title written on the front or on the spine.

Penelope closed her eyes for a moment. "Right," she muttered, turning to the first page.

Come into the Center

The Studies of Alpha Regius

So it did have a title after all—a very strange one. And what a strange name the author had too. Who was Alpha Regius? She started to leaf through the book. First there was a picture, but Penelope could only hazard a guess at what it was supposed to represent. It looked a bit like a wheel around which, somehow, many people were being whirled. In the center of this wheel was a figure with hands spread.

On the next page was another picture. Again, something that looked like a wheel, with a lot of people around it, and in the center a quiet figure that wasn't moving, just standing still. On the third page, another wheel with a figure in the middle, and on the fourth page, another.

This was all very odd. A little disappointed, Penelope continued to leaf through the pages, and was surprised when, after five more wheel pictures, she turned to a list of contents:

Come into the Center—Part One

On seeing

On realness

On friendship

Penelope's eyes scanned the lines, searching for . . . well, she didn't know what, but she was pretty sure it wasn't a recipe for ointment. Maybe some kind of clue that would tell her about her father. Perhaps *On seeing* would tell her how she could see him?

She flicked to the relevant page and blinked. Green-gold letters scrambled wildly across the paper, interspersed with silvery-blue vine illustrations, growing across the page as if they were alive. Penelope couldn't make out a single word, sentence, line, or any kind of context. No wonder G.E. couldn't figure out this book!

She was about to turn the page when something changed. Whether it was down to her eyes or the page, she couldn't say—but all of a sudden, the letters made sense:

Behind what's behind, always lies what's before,

You need the below, if above you wish to soar.

Well, this was better: Even though Penelope didn't understand yet what the writing meant, at least it was in full sentences now. She read the lines again, this time aloud: *"Behind what's behind, always lies what's before. You need the below, if above you wish to soar."* She felt the sound of the words inside herself, sensed them striking a chord within her.

Suddenly—and Penelope could have sworn they weren't there before—she spotted some more words on the bottom corner of the page:

To see through the eyes of another:

"Hex videris"

"Hex videris?" Penelope murmured. *"Hex videris . . .* sounds weird." *To see through the eyes of another*—that

was a bit easier to understand than all this "behind" and "before" stuff. Perhaps she could try looking around the kitchen through Granny Elizabeth's eyes—maybe she could just call out "*Hex videris!*" and then she could see for herself if the sink needed cleaning. Penelope giggled softly, then returned to the contents page, running her finger along the lines.

On rain training

That sounded interesting.

On shadow training

That sounded even more interesting.

On forgetting

On going back

On the invisible

Every single chapter sounded so interesting!

On wealth

On flying

On flying? Penelope's heart leapt. She flicked through the book rapidly, searching for the page. Hopefully she'd be able to make out the letters, hopefully she would understand. She was suddenly so excited that she had to compose herself a little so she didn't tear the pages. And then she was there, on the page.

Her heart thundered in her chest. There were no pictures, no vines, no strange gold letters: In black text on a white background, clear and easy to read, stood the words:

> If you are the fire, and you want to be in the air,
> Take root in the ground until it calls you there.
> Pour the water down from the top,
> Close your eyes, and lift yourself off.

"Semus triokko!"

A light bulb flicked on in Penelope's head. Of course—this explained everything! *Pour the water down from the top*... her lake-sodden hair must've been the difference between her first few attempts at flight and her ability to rise up into the trees. So *that* was it! You just needed water to complete the whole thing, to complete the four elements: fire, air, earth, and water!

"I'll try that," Penelope said to herself. "But not right now. Tomorrow. And not in here, or I might hit my head on the ceiling."

She hid the precious book under her mattress, got ready for bed, and went to sleep, exhausted.

17

Seeing

Why does time move about eighty times slower at school? Penelope had often wondered. And right now, as well as wrestling with this philosophical question, she was also pondering the age-old math puzzle: *How much longer till the bell rings?*

Even though Mr. Potts was possibly the nicest teacher in the world, Penelope simply couldn't summon up any enthusiasm for his math lessons. What was the *point* of learning all this stuff? What would anyone ever need to use it for? When would she finally be able to get out of here? Out and home to Alpha Regius, and then later to the stone circle, with a large bottle of water in her backpack and—

"Penelope?"

"Yes?"

"What do you mean, 'Yes'?" boomed Mr. Potts.

"Er . . . I thought you just said my name?"

"That's correct. I did say your name."

"And . . . er, why?" asked Penelope.

"Why? Now there's a question, my dear. And it could just possibly have something to do with the fact that I would like an answer from you."

"Seven point nine two," said Penelope. That was the figure written on the piece of paper that Pete was holding up behind the teacher's back.

"Very good, Penelope. You never cease to amaze me," said Mr. Potts approvingly. "That really was a very good bit of reading! And of course I must give a shout-out to our Pete for his accurate transcription, not to mention his beautiful handwriting!"

Penelope went red, and Pete looked down in embarrassment. Mr. Potts had obviously been practicing seeing through the eyes of another as well.

When school was finally over, and Penelope was eating dinner with her mother and Granny Elizabeth, there was a knock at the door of the dragon house. It was the postman. "Sorry, running a bit late today," he said. He plonked a parcel on the table. "Here's another heavy package for the esteemed Mrs. Elizabeth Burke, and here's the rest of your post." He smiled, wished them a good day, and was gone again.

The day's post included a rehab center authorization for Granny Elizabeth, who had visited the doctor after her dizzy spell in the field. A rest cure was when somebody went away and rested in order to improve their health, and Granny was to go to the coast in a month's time. She seemed rather pleased about it, but not as pleased as Penelope was. A three-week rest cure for her grandmother meant three weeks of intensive studies for Penelope, for she'd be able to spend hours on end putting her Alpha Regius studies to the test. What a wonderful thought!

"I'm going out," Penelope called to her mother after she'd finished her homework. She stuffed a large bottle of water into her backpack and opened the front door.

"Goodbye, my darling. I'll probably be at my rehearsal by the time you get back," Mrs. Gardener said, fetching a baseball cap from the table and handing it to Penelope. "Take some sun protection, please. Oh, and did you borrow my scarf? The one with the roses on? I've been looking for it for ages, and I can't seem to find it anywhere."

"Your scarf?" Penelope had hung it back on the clothes hook after she'd found it in the swamp forest, hadn't she? "Umm, no, I haven't borrowed it. But ask Granny—she's pretty good at 'borrowing' other people's things." Penelope hopped down the wooden steps.

"Penelope?"

"Yes?"

"Please be careful."

Penelope swallowed and nodded. Did she have *I'm going flying now* written across her forehead or something? Sometimes it was as if her mother could see right into her head.

18

Finally Flying!

The heat had parched the ground, turning the grass around the stone circle into stalks of straw. Sweat poured down Penelope's face and stung her eyes. It would have been more comfortable to practice in the shade, of course, but shade meant trees—and Penelope definitely didn't want to risk another collision.

Setting her baseball cap on the ground, she opened her backpack and took out her water bottle. Now she was ready. She stood in the middle of the stone circle, slowly unscrewed the cap of the bottle, and held it above her head, ready to pour.

"Ready?" she said aloud. "Yes? OK, let's go!" She closed her eyes and concentrated on her feet, rooting them in the hard, dry ground. She felt the soles of her feet tingle, braced herself for the electric shock running through her body, then poured most of the water over her head. *"Semus triokko!"* she shouted.

Her feet lifted off the ground, slowly at first, then gathering speed until she was shooting upward like an arrow. The wind rushed past Penelope's ears, the air temperature around her dropping sharply. Her stomach somersaulted as she glanced down, the landscape below her growing smaller, the buildings quickly as tiny as dollhouses. Wispy clouds scudded past, but still she kept climbing. She needed to figure out how to stop, or she'd never get back to the ground—or else she'd have turned into an ice cube by the time she did.

Grasping the bottle in one hand, she reached quickly into her hair with the other and pulled. Immediately she lurched forward onto her belly, her body spinning around on its own axis, but she was still climbing upward. Penelope dropped the bottle and reached into her hair with both hands, pulling desperately.

Tschschsch! Her upward trajectory finally ground to a halt. She gave a sigh of relief. She was so high now that the icy mountain air hurt her lungs. All she could see of the world below her was a faint gray-green haze, veiled by clouds.

"Holy swamp cow, why is nothing ever straightforward?" she complained. "And why does everything have to be so extreme?" Shivering with cold, she pulled her hair again and began her descent. Gradually, the stone circle reappeared, and she was back in the warmth of summer. She gently lifted her hands from her hair and paused midair, lying on her front, then waved herself forward—the movement was like swimming, really—and immediately slid along like a fish.

Interesting! Now that Penelope was lying on her front, she found she could fly through the air like a red feather, slow, weightless, and silent. She propelled herself forward. The meadow flew past, then a field of corn, and then a field of rapeseed. She flew over rows of cabbages—a hare bounding energetically between the lines—and skimmed the tops of whitethorn and hazelnut hedges. She saw a pair of ducks waddling in a dried-out pond and waved to them as she flew on over a pine wood and out the other side, where horses stood motionless in the sun. Fields of red poppies and blue cornflowers flashed by, their colors vivid against the parched ground. Penelope gaped in wonder, a quiet joy spreading through her: Viewed from up here, the world was simply, dazzlingly beautiful.

A flock of birds suddenly appeared on her flight path. Instinctively, Penelope pulled on one side of her still-damp hair, and immediately turned in that direction. She chuckled: This was so easy!

"Did you see that?" she called out to the birds. "Now, that's what I call super-strength hair control!"

The birds flew off, ignoring Penelope's new discovery. But that didn't matter, because Penelope just pulled her hair again and flew after them.

"It's a special edition—it's called Galactic Penelope! You might find it useful too. I'll try and get you some, if you like."

The birds didn't like: They made another sharp U-turn and flew toward the herd of horses, but Penelope kept following, as smoothly as a veil drawn through water. Before the birds reached the pine woods, they started to descend. Penelope flew very low and made a slightly bumpy landing in the middle of a cornfield.

Laughing, she plopped down onto the dry ground, stretched out her arms and legs, and looked up at the sky through the pine trees. *I was up there*, she thought. *I was right—I was right! I can do it, just like the birds—I can go up, I can go straight, I can come down.* There was a choir singing a hymn in her heart. But suddenly, the conductor of this choir gave the signal for "total silence," and Penelope sat up with a start.

"The bottle! I've got no water left!"

She hadn't thought this through properly. She should never have landed here, because without water, she couldn't get high enough to fly back. She was going to have to walk back home—and it was a long, long way on foot. Grimly, she pushed the sharp corn leaves apart and started to work her way through the field.

By the time she arrived back at the dragon house late at night, Galactic Penelope was aching all over.

19

Two Letters

Tom and Pete were so fidgety the next morning at school that they fell off their chairs twice during the German lesson, and ended up getting black marks from Mrs. Norton. Penelope, on the other hand, sat completely motionless at her table, far too tired to even move, let alone fidget. She was still aching and exhausted after yesterday's long walk home. If Anna-Lea hadn't nudged her and pushed a small folded note onto her desk, she would quite possibly have fallen asleep and got herself a black mark too. She unfolded the note, curious. She instantly felt better, because it read:

Hey, Pen, my uncle's just started working at the multiplex cinema in the Ring Center. I've got a bunch of free tickets for tomorrow. All the films, all day. And unlimited popcorn and ice cream. Fancy a trip to town? My mom will drive us there, and Pete's dad's picking us up afterward. We're setting off at 10.

Tom

A trip into town with Tom and Pete, and as many films as she wanted? Penelope smiled and wrote back, *I'm in*. But she didn't pass the note back to Anna-Lea—instead, she screwed it up and threw it when Mrs. Norton's back was turned. It hit Pete squarely on the forehead. Pete jumped, grinned, and pushed the note over to Tom as Mrs. Norton turned back to the class. Penelope wrote, *Die Katze frisst nicht die Spinne* in her exercise book with an angelic expression on her face.

She hurried home after school. There was a lot to do: First of all, she wanted to ask her mother about tomorrow's movie theater excursion, and then there was the problem of the water bottle to solve—how could she guarantee a steady supply of water when she flew? She also wanted to see if she could find an ointment recipe anywhere in the Alpha Regius book. That would make G.E. happy, and besides, Penelope could do with something like that herself after yesterday's exhausting walk home. She was covered in scrapes and bruises.

Granny Elizabeth was kneeling down in the vegetable patch in front of the dragon house, between the celery and the carrots, doing some weeding. She looked up as Penelope hopped up the wooden steps. "Ah, there you are. You can give me a hand. Lucia needs some peace and quiet, and I'm going to tackle these dratted creeper corms. As it's hardly rained this year, maybe we can knock them on the head once and for all. The pointed shovel's over there," she said, tugging at a stubborn root.

"Maybe later, Granny!" Penelope called out cheerfully. She had no intention of doing any weeding right now. She wanted to tell her mother about Tom's movie theater vouchers first, even if she did need peace and quiet. She quickly slipped into the house before Granny could protest.

"Mooooom! Guess what happened today?"

Her mother was sitting at the kitchen table, staring at the wall.

"Mom?" Penelope put her backpack down and went over to the table. Her mother didn't say anything, but simply nodded to the envelope in front of her. A gray envelope with a sticker on it.

"Has he only sent five dollars again?" Penelope's lip trembled slightly. She didn't want to think that the man who was her father could do such a thing.

"No," said her mother tonelessly. "He's sent sand."

"Sand?"

"Yes. Sand and feathers. Look in the envelope. That's what he expects us to live on this month."

Penelope took the envelope. She could feel little grains through the paper.

"If I could get my hands on that man, I'd . . ." whispered her mother. "Why can't he just stop this? He can keep his stupid money as far as I'm concerned—I can manage without it. But why does he have to torment me like this? Hasn't he got anything better to do? What's he getting out of all this? I've never done anything to hurt him. Never. I don't understand . . . we loved each other so much."

Penelope was at a loss for words. She didn't understand it either. She wanted to comfort her mother, but had no idea how. Her chest felt tight; in the same spot where music and happiness had been only yesterday, a choking feeling was taking root. The feeling spread through her lungs. Penelope had never felt so full of rage, had never felt such an uncontrollable fury as she felt toward the man who had sent this envelope. And that anger drove her upstairs and into her room, where she pulled the book out from its hiding place under the mattress.

I'll find something in here. Something that will hurt you, Leo Gardener. I swear it.

Her hands shaking, she leafed past the wheel pictures in search of the book's contents page, but there was nothing but grayish pages tangled with green tendrils, one after another.

"Fine. I don't need the contents. I can find what I need myself!" She carried on turning the pages, trembling, but every one was identical to the last.

She remembered last time—how the words had bloomed gradually before her eyes. "OK, I get it. I've got to wait," she growled, and stared grimly at the green shoots. "Well, get on with it, then." She stared and stared, but nothing happened. "OK, then, just forget it!" The book clattered onto the floorboards. "To heck with you, Alpha Regius—I'll find some way of getting back at him without your help." She stared out of the window with a poisonous look on her face. "I need a few good ideas, that's all."

But the good ideas would have to wait. Good ideas didn't like anger, Penelope knew that—they tended to keep their distance until the anger had spent itself. But that just made Penelope even madder. She looked around the room wildly, searching for something she could break.

She heard a meow outside her bedroom door. She opened it, shouted, "Push off, Coco!" and was about to slam the door shut, but Coco had already squeezed her way in and was looking at Penelope so scathingly that she had to bite her lip.

The cat sat down next to the book on the floor and stuck her nose in the air. She sneezed, then jumped onto the bed and gazed into Penelope's eyes expectantly. Penelope looked away at first, but after a while, she picked the book up off the floor and laid it on the table. "Happy now?" she grumbled. Coco yawned, turned around several times on the spot, and sank into the cushions. Penelope waited, but the cat ignored her.

"What is it *now*?"

Coco was washing her back vigorously.

Penelope sat down on the bed. Coco just carried on washing.

"OK, OK. I'm sorry."

Immediately a paw landed in her lap. That meant: *Apology accepted, you may stroke me now.* Penelope didn't need telling twice. She stroked the gray fur, again and again, her heart calming a little every time she moved her hand over Coco's sleek coat. The last traces of her anger faded away and finally vanished altogether. And as Coco licked her hand, Penelope saw the first glimmer of a plan taking shape in her mind's eye.

She had to go to Blackslough. There were no two ways about it. She had to go there and track down her father and stop him from tormenting her mother any longer. Finding him might be rather difficult, without an exact address—but then again, maybe it wouldn't be too difficult, for in a month's time her father would send another of his gray envelopes. They always arrived on the seventh . . .

Penelope would go to Blackslough the day before, then, on the sixth of July. She'd camp out at the post office. No—first she'd have to make sure all the postboxes in the village were out of order. Some superglue might do the job . . . yes, she would glue up the flaps on all the postboxes—except the one at the post office. Then anyone in the village who wanted to send anything on the sixth of July would have to use that one. Then all Penelope would have to do was wait. If a man came along and posted a letter in a dark gray envelope, she'd follow him. She'd trail him back to his house and then she would . . . Penelope glanced out the window at Granny weeding the front garden. That's it, she would throw creeper corms into his yard! It would be perfect. If he didn't weed them out right away, they'd overgrow his whole house and yard, clinging to the walls and slowly destroying his foundations.

Or she could pour sand into his letter box. Or she could paint his windowpanes gray and leave some of her red hairs drying in the paint. Or . . . she could simply ring the doorbell.

Yes. That was it. She'd pour water over her head, ring the doorbell, and say, "I'm Penelope Gardener!" She'd look at him through narrowed eyes. "If you think your gray envelopes are funny, you're wrong. In the future, you can keep your money and build sandcastles with your stupid sand, for all we care!" Perhaps her father would take a breath and start to say something, but Penelope would be quicker. "Save your apologies for someone who wants to hear them." Then she would simply turn around and walk away.

"Penelope! Wait, please!" Her father was bound to follow her, but she wouldn't stop. Maybe he'd say something else, but she wouldn't listen. She would have already taken root, shouted, *"Semus triokko!"* and taken off into the sky. She'd leave him behind, his words crumbling to dust around him. And then she'd throw the creeper corms down, too, for good measure.

Yes. That was a better plan. But in order to carry it out, she'd have to:

Find out where this Blackslough was, and how to get there.

Dye her hair gray again. She didn't want her father to sense her presence before she rang the bell, after all—that would totally defeat the purpose.

Buy some brown hair dye to cover the gray, because her father would be sure to notice a gray-haired child at the post office. And he'd know exactly how she came to have hair like that—he was the one who'd made the ash paste, after all.

"Pennyyyyy!" Mrs. Gardener's warm voice echoed up the stairs. "You said you wanted to tell me something. Come down, let's not let that idiot ruin our day."

Oh, yes—Penelope still hadn't said anything to her mother about the movie theater trip tomorrow. Her heart lightened at the thought—plus, she realized, she'd be able to buy some brown hair dye at the shopping center. The movie marathon really was a double stroke of luck.

20

Movie Marathon

The next day at eleven o'clock, Penelope was standing with Tom and Pete on a very long escalator, traveling up to the movie theater. The Ring Center was an enormous glass complex, with lots of shops, restaurants, hair salons, and cafés, crowned by a multiscreen movie theater on the top floor.

"We've definitely got to see *Killer Whale 3* first," said Tom, grinning from ear to ear.

"Stuff that," said Pete. "We're starting with either *Horror Fighter* or *The Mushrooms of Terror*, like we agreed."

Penelope was beginning to wonder whether a

movie marathon with the two boys had been such a great idea, but suddenly they both snorted. "Just kidding. We know we're in the presence of a lady." The boys laughed uproariously, leaning on the escalator railing. But when she said, "Well, in that case, I think we should see *The Moon Dust Fairy Finds Her Magic Pony*." They grew oddly silent, and Penelope smirked behind her hand.

On arriving at the movie theater, they finally settled unanimously on *Storm on the High Seas* as their first film, and settled down with cups of slush in the huge, almost empty theater. The film was a bit boring, Tom and Pete started a running commentary on the actors' hairstyles and noses, and Penelope found herself cracking up with laughter. She really liked Tom, and she really liked Pete, but as a double act, they were simply unbeatable. They had the knack of making almost anything seem funny. But the boys were quiet during the next film, *Save Yourselves from Soramo*, as that one was totally gripping. Penelope almost grabbed Pete's hand during one especially exciting bit, but she pulled herself together.

Later they recovered with popcorn in the foyer.

Penelope's heart was still beating a little faster than usual, and the noises around her seemed far too loud. Tom stuffed a handful of popcorn into his mouth and wiped his fingers on his jeans. "Hey, look—*The Lord of the Seven Kingdoms* is starting in a minute. Shall we get some more ice cream and go back in?"

"I could do with a bit of a break, guys," said Penelope decisively. "Why don't you go and see the killer whale film? I'll go for a bit of a wander round the shops, and we can meet up again at five, maybe?"

Tom and Pete pretended to be indignant, but Penelope could tell from the way their eyes lit up that the killer whale idea was a winner. Penelope took the escalator down to the shops and walked along past windows full of garish clothes, jewelry, and stationery. *I'd just better watch I don't get lost in here*, she thought.

The next moment, a fleeting shiver suddenly passed across the back of her neck and ran down her spine.

Someone like me!

Penelope spun round. There was someone around here somewhere who was the same as her! Her curiosity started to fight her caution—she had longed to find someone like her, someone to advise her and answer her questions . . . she *had* to speak to them! They were really close by too—she could feel it. But where? There were so many people pushing past her that it was difficult to tell. She looked to the left, to the right, she rocked up onto the tips of her toes. She tried to gaze into the eyes of the passersby, but far from their eyes lighting up as they recognized one of their own, people appeared to be unnerved. The person like her was growing farther away, not closer, the feeling was weakening, and suddenly it vanished altogether. Penelope felt sad and frustrated, as if she'd lost something precious. She waited, scanning the crowd, but she couldn't feel anyone.

After a while, she gave up. She carried on browsing the shops until a shoe shop caught her eye. It had shoelaces in the window—shoelaces in all the colors of the rainbow! Less than a minute later, she was the proud owner of a pair of electric-blue laces. She'd finally be able to give Pete his shoelace back.

She glanced at the clock. She had quite a while

before five, when she'd promised to meet up with Tom and Pete. Plenty of time to locate a pharmacy in the huge complex, and buy a packet of brown hair dye.

Penelope eventually found herself in the pharmacy on the ground floor, but as she scanned the endless shelf of hair dyes, she started to wonder whether she had enough time after all. Choosing between light, medium, and dark brown was just the start—how on earth was she supposed to choose between Mahogany Brown, Chestnut Brown, Rust Brown, Cocoa Brown, Lanzarote Brown, Alder Brown, and Hazel Brown? Or what about Icelandic Earth Brown?

She took a box of Icelandic Earth Brown off the shelf, and was about to read the back of it, when her neck tingled again, and a fleeting tremor passed down her spine. Before Penelope could turn around to find the person like her, someone tapped her on the shoulder.

"I don't believe it!" exclaimed a girl's voice. "We've been living here for three years, and I've never met a single person of our kind until now!"

A slender girl with strawberry-blond hair, a little taller than Penelope, was standing opposite her. She was wearing a bottle-green dress and ankle boots, and was staring at Penelope through pale, close-set eyes.

"Where have you sprung from all of a sudden?" asked the girl. But all Penelope could do was stare openmouthed at the girl, too tongue-tied to reply. *Someone like me!* she kept thinking excitedly. *Someone who could help explain . . . everything!*

"Are you just visiting or do you live here? Why are you looking at hair coloring stuff—does it work on you, then? Nothing happened whatsoever when I tried it. My mom said that was normal for people like us—the color just won't go in, no matter what you do. And one time my brother tried . . . Oh, I'm sorry, I haven't even introduced myself. I'm Gina. What's your name?" The girl held out a slim, pale hand to Penelope.

"Penelope," she managed to say, slowly coming out of her trance. She reached for the girl's hand and shook it.

21

Gina

"That's an interesting name. So, what's up?"

"I'm here with my friends," Penelope said. "We're having a movie marathon—but I'm skipping the killer whale movie."

"It's so cool to finally meet one of us! Hey, want to come back to my place for a bit? I mean, I know we've only just met, but I live right round the corner and it would be cool to talk properly without, you know . . ." She waved her hand at the crowds of people in the shopping center.

If anyone else had asked her that, Penelope might have tapped her forehead and said, "Excuse me? I've known you for exactly three seconds. Why would I want to come back to yours?" But it was different with this Gina: Penelope *wanted* to go with her, to see what her house was like, and her family, and her *world*. The girl was certainly peculiar, but that was the point: Penelope was peculiar too, and she'd never met anyone else like that.

"OK. But I've got to be back up at the movie theater by five. My friends will be waiting for me," she said.

"Friends? Are they . . . ?" A slightly greedy expression came over Gina's face, then vanished immediately as Penelope shook her head. "Oh, well, I guess that would be a bit much, all in one day. Anyway, we can get you back here for five, no worries. Like I said, I live really close by." She tucked a strand of hair behind her ear, linked her arm through Penelope's, and pulled her toward the checkout. Penelope paid for the hair dye, and then Gina led her out of the Ring Center and toward a large apartment building across the road.

On the way, Gina asked Penelope so many questions that her head began to ache. She answered the non-stop stream as best she could; she told Gina that she hardly ever came to town and that up until a short time ago, her hair hadn't even been like this. She didn't really want to explain that any further—after all, even though Gina was just like her, that didn't mean Penelope had to spill the beans on *everything*. But she did tell her that she'd inherited her hair, and other things, from her father, and that she didn't know him. In turn, Gina told Penelope that she and her family felt a little bit lonely living here. It was easier for her brother, Gian, because he was already fourteen, so he could go on "courses" during school breaks.

"What kind of courses?" asked Penelope.

"Well, there are these training courses run by the Alpha Regius people. They don't let you start till you're eleven. Don't you think that's stupid? But I've already taught myself a whole bunch of stuff, and . . . oh, hi, Mrs. Jaluschek." Gina nodded to an old lady who was just coming out of the glass door of an apartment block, said, "Sorry, no time to chat right now!" and pulled Penelope by the arm into a rather dingy stairwell.

"Who is Alpha Regius?" Penelope asked, recognizing the name from her book.

Gina's eyebrows rose up.

"Is? Who *was* Alpha Regius would be the better question. He isn't alive anymore, but he started the whole training thing."

Before Penelope could ask any other questions, they rode up to the eighth floor in a lift that smelled of cigarette smoke. Penelope could feel the shiver on the back of her neck again, much more strongly than before. *More people like me!*

Gina was just about to unlock the door to her flat when it flew open of its own accord. A tall freckled lady with a black sun hat in her hand stood in the doorway, beaming.

"Oh, Gina! You've brought a guest! Wonderful, that's wonderful—come in, you two. I must say, it's very refreshing to see someone like us around here. Would you like some lemonade? Or would you prefer juice? Of course, there's coffee as well . . . I could put some ice cream out . . . would you like some cherries to take up to your room? Or . . . no, you must come and sit with me on the balcony—I'll put the shade on it so we don't get too hot. Gian is in his room, we'll fetch him, too, of course—and then, my dear fire-red child, you must tell us where you—"

"Mom!" Gina flashed a look at her mother.

"Oh, I beg your pardon! I'm sorry. Of course, I understand—you girls want to be alone. So, just give me a shout if you need anything, and if you do want to come and join me on the balcony, then . . . um, yes, OK, I'll just . . ." She darted down the hallway and disappeared behind a door.

"I can't blame her." Gina shrugged. "I think it's really exciting that we've found you too."

Penelope smiled, feeling a little embarrassed. She had so many questions, but somehow she felt too overwhelmed to ask anything at all!

Gina's room was incredible. Not that Penelope found

it strange that someone should have a silver-painted bed and a black bedspread, a large dark blue rug with a silver spiral pattern, a black wooden writing desk, a dainty shelf painted with cobwebs, and a cupboard with a mirror on it. What really struck her about the room was that it was as clean and tidy as a set piece in a furniture store. There was nothing lying around, not a speck of dust to be seen, the bed was neatly made up without a single wrinkle. The books were arranged on the shelf by color, the pens and pencils were all neatly stored in a pot on the desk, and the windows were so clean it was impossible to tell if there was actually glass in the frames.

"This is your room?" Penelope was amazed. Even though she hadn't known her long, Gina didn't seem like the kind of person to keep her room so neat and clean.

"Yes. You can come in, you know—it's quite safe," answered Gina, sitting down cross-legged on the shaggy rug.

Penelope came into the room and stood around, feeling a little awkward. "It's pretty tidy in here. My room never looks this tidy," she said in amazement.

"Mine never used to either," Gina giggled. "That's why Gian gave me automatic room cleaning for my last birthday. He'd just learned it on his latest course and he was able to use it straightaway, thanks to me being so messy."

"What, your room tidies itself, you mean? That's handy." Penelope's eyes shone at the thought.

"It's more than handy. But I'm actually really glad the self-cleaning doesn't last forever. It wears off after five months—at least I'll be able to get some sleep then." Gina sank down on the rug with a sigh, curled herself up in a ball, and closed her eyes with dramatic slowness.

"What has sleep got to do with tidying up?" asked Penelope, puzzled.

"Oh, nothing really. It's just that Gian's creation isn't exactly what you'd call flexible. Every weekend, my duvet throws me out of bed at six thirty in the morning so it can shake itself out and then air itself by the open window for an hour."

"What?" Penelope giggled.

"It does it no matter what the weather's like. I've often ended up with a soaking wet pillow that Mom's had to dry off for me."

"But apart from that, it must be amazing to have that sort of room service, surely?"

"Pretty much. Want to see how it works?" Without waiting for a reply, Gina jumped up, slipped out of the room, and came back with a full vacuum cleaner bag. She held it over the dark blue rug and began to shake the contents out vigorously. Dirt, dust, sand, and hair spilled out, covering the rug with a thick, disgusting layer of filth.

"Now we've got to wait for a bit," she informed Penelope, pulling her onto the bed. "You can tell me a bit about yourself in the meantime. Like, what have you taught yourself so far? What can you do?"

Penelope stared at the filthy rug. Was the dirt simply going to disappear?

"Hey, forget about the rug and tell me what you can do." Gina tugged at Penelope's sleeve insistently.

Penelope hesitated. She didn't really know what to say—what was normal? Should she really be talking about this with other people?

"Can't you do anything yet?" Gina asked, with a mixture of disappointment and sympathy in her voice. "Oh, well, never mind. Anyway—"

"I can hear the road," Penelope mumbled finally.

"Yes, there's always a lot of traffic at this time of day. It's not as bad in the evenings, though."

"No, no, I don't mean the cars," said Penelope. "I mean the actual road. I can hear it talking to me."

Gina's mouth twisted into a puzzled smile. "The road talks? Seriously?"

"Yes. It saved me from an out-of-control tractor once, and it helped me learn to fly."

Gina hesitated for a second and then burst out

laughing. "You crack me up, Penelope. How cool would that be? If only we really could. But Mom once met someone at a seminar who really did manage to get into the air. He got about a foot and a half up, or maybe even a bit higher than that. Just imagine! Of course, he was some kind of super-expert with super-dark red hair and, oh, I don't know, about a million years' training. Perhaps with Alpha Regius personally. No idea. We'd never be able to manage it, of course. But seriously, that thing with the road is quite interesting. How do you do that, then? And if you—?"

Sensing that what she'd suggested wasn't quite normal, Penelope was rather relieved when the rug began to vibrate crazily and Gina stopped talking to watch. The rug folded itself up, again and again, until it was just a tiny square. A moment later, the window opened by itself, and the rug jumped onto the windowsill. It unfolded itself and started to shake like mad. Dirt flew out in dense grayish-brown clouds and floated down to the street below. Then the rug laid itself back in place on the floor. Little foam bubbles formed on its surface and rubbed themselves into the fibers in circular movements. Then a few tiny fountains spurted on, and finally Penelope could hear a noise that sounded like a hair dryer.

"What do you think of that, then? Cool or what?"

Gina slid off the bed and sat back down on the rug, which was now immaculately clean. Penelope was about to do the same when her eye fell on Gina's wastepaper basket. It was empty apart from a small round silver object.

"What's that in the bin?"

"Oh, that's just rubbish—that's why I threw it away. But my room doesn't recognize it as rubbish, so the thing stays in the bin when it empties itself. It's as if it was a magnet and the bin was made of metal."

"O . . . K . . . But what is it?"

"It's an Anti-Eye."

"What's it for?"

"That's just it—it's not working anymore. Gian brought it back from a seminar for me." Gina took the little tin box out of the wastepaper basket and put it in Penelope's hand. "See that rusty button there? If you press it, you disappear. Well, you really just become invisible, obviously. The effect is meant to last for half an hour. Trouble is, it's broken, so you only stay invisible for ten seconds. What use is that? It's not even long enough to nick any sweets from Mom's stash."

Penelope wasn't really listening to her anymore. She couldn't help it—immediately she found her thumb drawn toward the button. Just as Gina was saying, "But don't press it," Penelope vanished.

Penelope stared at the place where her hand had just been holding the little box. There was simply nothing there. No hand, no box—nothing but thin air. Her thighs were invisible too; there was nothing but a flattened semicircle on the bedcover where they had been. Wow! No sooner had Penelope grasped what had happened to her than the ten seconds were over, and her body was back, sitting on the bed as if nothing had happened at all.

"That's amazing," she whispered. She cleared her throat and tried again. "That's amazing!" she said, but her voice was so quiet that even she could barely hear it.

Gina grinned. "Yes. But I told you not to press it!"

"Sorry," whispered Penelope.

"You've really done it now! You won't be able to talk any louder than a whisper for—I think it might be ten minutes. I did tell you it was broken."

"Oh," whispered Penelope. "That doesn't matter—the invisibility thing is really exciting."

"Would you like it? Take it, I really don't need it anymore. Gian can bring me a new one sometime."

"I can keep it? Really? I mean—thanks!"

"What did you say?" Gina had to come a little closer, as Penelope's whisper was getting quieter by the second.

"Thanks," Penelope breathed.

"I can't hear you. And it's five past five—you're going to have to shake a leg if you don't want to keep your mates hanging around forever."

Penelope leapt up. She couldn't believe how fast time had passed!

"You can come over again next time you're in town," Gina said. "I'll show you all the stuff Gian's put on my phone, stuff he's learned at seminars."

Penelope smiled and nodded, and they exchanged numbers. Gina walked her back to the elevator, and then Penelope was alone again, descending to the ground floor.

22

Bad Fortune

As Penelope stepped outside, a lady in an elegant white dress, with a pug in her arms, was standing in front of a metallic gold convertible in front of Gina's house—the whole car was covered in dust. "I'm telling you, this town is the pits!" she was screeching into a cell phone. "The dirt in this place . . . what's just happened to me would never happen in our neighborhood. You wouldn't believe what the car looks like now—the windshield, the white upholstery, all of it is completely filthy! Oh, no, there's no way we're buying anything around here, it'd be the world's worst investment . . .

OK . . . good, see you at the hotel. Horst and I desperately need to take a bath and wash our hair and . . ."

Penelope grinned to herself: Gina's rug had really made a mess of the lady's car.

She ran quickly past the woman, who was still ranting into her phone, and crossed the road to the Ring Center. It took her a while to find the escalators when she got there; she looked up and saw Tom and Pete a long way above, obviously searching for her.

Hey, you two, I'm on my way! she tried to shout. But all that came out of her mouth was a soft hissing noise.

She ran up one escalator after another, shouting "Anti-Eye!" each time she got onto a different one, to test whether her voice had come back yet. She managed a loud whisper after the third, and on the fifth she finally managed to make a sound.

"Pete, Pete, here she comes! I can see her. Our wise Penelope is walking this way!" Tom leaned over the glass railing and waved to her, laughing.

Penelope stepped from the last escalator into the movie theater foyer. Pete danced around her. "Penny, you had the right idea, giving that pile of rubbish a swerve. Hello?! Not a single drop of blood, just some stupid baby whales that had some kind of chickenpox. One of them got bitten, and that drew a load of slimy snorkel fish to them, that all looked like Mr. Potts, and—"

"Dude, *you* look like Mr. Potts. Hey, Penny, how was it? How was . . . ? Well, what did you get up to?" Tom held his popcorn out to her.

Penelope reached into the bag, looking from one of them to the other. She cleared her throat, her voice finally returned. "I bought a pair of blue shoelaces and some hair dye, and I met a girl who's the same as me."

"No way!" exclaimed Pete.

"She can't be the same as you, or we'd already be friends with her," Tom shouted.

"Exactly. Anyway, there could never be two Penelopes." That was Pete again. Penelope smiled.

"But look, we need to shake a leg now," Tom shouted, jumping onto the downward escalator. Pete and Penelope followed him down to the elevators. Pete's father would already be waiting on parking deck three, as arranged, so Tom was right: They'd have to hurry!

"Here comes the film club," Pete's dad greeted them, smiling, as they got out of the elevator in the car park. He looked different from the last time Penelope had seen him—less jolly. In fact, he seemed quite stressed.

"All aboard, everyone," he said. "Enjoy your last ride in the Bentley—it's being sold tomorrow."

"But Dad! You said you wouldn't sell the car!" cried Pete in dismay.

"I know, my dear son, but that's all changed, sadly. The business is really going downhill now, you know that. Things were going so well at the start of this year, but now . . ." Pete's dad shook his head as he ushered the children into the back seats. "I just can't understand what's going on—it's as if there's a jinx on the place." He slid into the driver's seat, buckled up, and started the engine. "On Monday, I'm going to have to start letting people go, and if things don't pick up soon, I'll have to close down by the end of the year."

"But what will you do then? How are we going to manage?" Pete was clearly upset.

"Oh, I can always get a job. And Mom can go back to work too. Don't worry, we'd manage—we'd just have to cut back on the luxuries, that's all. Honestly, nothing to worry about!" Pete's dad smiled at his son in the rearview mirror—but it was obvious to Penelope that the smile was forced.

23

Battling with Vegetables

Over the next few weeks, Penelope tried again and again to read some more of the Alpha Regius book, but it wasn't easy. Sometimes it seemed that the harder she tried, and the more frustrated she grew, the less she could see. When she was calm, she could still make out the pictures with the wheels, and the chapters on flying and seeing with the eyes of another, but on most of the other pages, all she could see were the dainty pale blue vines with silvery veins, peculiar-looking animal heads, or ugly laughing faces scrambled between the green-gold letters that danced across the page, as if taunting her. The words didn't seem to want to show themselves, apart from a lonely golden letter standing still here and there—and those weren't of much use to Penelope on their own. But she didn't give up—she kept leafing through the precious book every day, hoping that soon it would decide to reveal more.

When she wasn't occupied with her Alpha Regius book, she practiced flying, and when she wasn't practicing flying, she experimented with Gina's Anti-Eye. She wondered if it was possible somehow to fix the device and stay invisible for longer, and perhaps she could find a remedy for the hoarseness that occurred every time she pressed the rusty button on the little magic box.

Penelope was also preparing to confront her father face-to-face. After all, since her conversation with Gina, she knew he was very powerful, and she definitely didn't want to seem like some silly girl who'd only just figured out some of the basics. She ran through the journey to Blackslough again and again in her head. It was too far away, she thought, to risk trying to fly—and the village was small and not very well connected. She already knew that she had to take the bus to the train station in Senborough, where she had been with her mom several times. She'd wait a while at the station, and catch the train to a place called Little Pilling. She'd have to walk across the countryside for a mile or two, and then she'd be in Blackslough. The journey would take about three and a half hours, so she was going to have to set off extremely early if she wanted to arrive in time to glue up the flaps on all the postboxes.

Now Penelope was sitting cross-legged on her bed. Whenever she wasn't thinking about her father during this time, she was thinking about Pete's father instead. Pete had been really upset—and his dad had been too, even though he'd been putting on a brave face. She wished she could find out why his company was losing so much money all of a sudden.

"Penelopeeeee!" Granny Elizabeth's voice wrenched

her from her thoughts. "Get down here. We need your help with the creeper corms!"

As if she had nothing better to do! Oh, well, never mind—it might do her good to take a break from all this incessant thinking. Besides, she could pack a couple of the ugliest specimens as a gift for her father.

She clattered down the wooden staircase. The front door was open. Granny Elizabeth and her mother were crouching behind the wild rosebush, both of them pulling at a particularly stubborn creeper corm root. Mrs. Gardener chuckled.

"You know, you're really getting a bit obsessed with these things, Mother."

"Make fun of me all you like, Lucia, but once we've got rid of the things, you'll see how much of a favor I've done us all." Granny Elizabeth was rather red in the face, but she seemed to be in a wonderful mood. "Ah, Penelope, there you are! Could you start digging just here, please? I think there's a massive one down there.

We're going to finish these creeper corms off today, you just see if we don't."

The problem with the creeper corms was their tangled, long roots: Due to the bristly tubers that formed at regular intervals along their lengths, it was very difficult to pull the plants out of the ground entirely. But it might be a bit easier now, Penelope realized as she picked up a spade, since the heat and the lack of rain had stopped the creeper corms from growing as enthusiastically this year. What's more, Granny Elizabeth seemed to have found the creeper's main root.

Penelope helped her mom and granny dig a deep hollow around the corm, and then all three of them pulled together, each gripping on to a different section of the sprawling root. They tugged and plucked and tore. At first, there wasn't much movement, but then there was a sudden jolt, and all three of them lost their grip and landed on the ground. Granny Elizabeth was the first to stand up. Immediately she started pulling at the loose earth. The roots were coming away quite easily now, and more and more of the creeper corms were emerging from the ground. Granny threw each tuber over her shoulder and they landed on the lawn, each connected to the next, forming a long lasso shape. Penelope and her mother started to help—and after a while, G.E. was actually holding the last traces of the stubborn weed in her hands! They measured the total length later on: sixty feet of connected tubers, with eight single and thirty-one twin corms.

"Hahaaa!" Granny Elizabeth raised her arms in triumph. For a moment, she looked like a young girl again. "We've finally done it! We've wiped out that awful weed at last! It's been sucking the life out of our plants for years on end, but it's finally had its comeuppance! Um, no pun intended." She bent down and began to spool up the roots as if they were a ball of wool. "Oh, but let's not throw the thing away. We'll dry it out and keep it in a box as a souvenir." She marched into the house, her chest inflated with pride.

No, we can't throw them away, thought Penelope, *but I can think of a much better use for them than keeping them in a box. As it's all come up in one piece, I'll take the whole thing with me when I pay my visit to Mr. Gray-Letter-Sender.*

Granny Elizabeth popped her head out of the window. "Lucia! Penelope! This calls for a celebration! I'll bake us a victory cake."

Penelope and her mother exchanged a brief glance. "Oh, there's no need to do that, Mother," Mrs. Gardener called out hastily. "It'd be quicker for Penelope to go and get us something from the baker's, don't you think?"

Cycling to the bakery wasn't exactly Penelope's favorite activity, but the prospect of having to eat one of Granny Elizabeth's cakes gave her an energy boost!

"EVERYTHING IS IN MOTION AGAIN," rumbled the road the minute Penelope's bike touched the pavement.

"What?"

"EVERYTHING IS FLOWING ALONG, EVERYTHING IS RUNNING SMOOTHLY. THE ROADBLOCKS HAVE

BEEN CLEARED. ONE OF MY OLDER MOTORWAYS HAS GAINED ANOTHER LANE, EVERYONE IS GETTING TO THEIR DESTINATION QUICKLY. THE WAIT IS OVER, EVERYTHING'S MOVING, AND I'M STILL HERE, AND WHERE WOULD YOU LIKE TO GO, MY DEAR CHILD?"

"To the baker's. Granny Elizabeth's conquered the creeper corms, so we're having cake to celebrate."

"UGH, CREEPER CORMS!" the road yelped. "THOSE ARE REALLY BAD GUYS. I HAD THOSE THINGS GROWING UP THROUGH ONE OF MY SOUTHERN BRANCHES FOR YEARS. AN EXTREMELY RARE PLANT, BUT ALSO A VERY UNPLEASANT ONE. AND THOSE TUBERS! OH, I KNOW THEY'RE VERY PRETTY AT FIRST, BUT IF THEY GROW TOO FAST, THEN—OUCH!—MY POOR ROAD! IT'S WORST DURING THE HAY SEASON. WHEN IT RAINS, AND THE HAY THAT FALLS ON ME MIXES WITH THE RAINWATER . . . IF ANY OF THAT GETS ONTO THE CREEPER CORMS, THEY LITERALLY EXPLODE! THEY SWELL UP AS BIG AS PUMPKINS SOMETIMES. OH, YES, IT'S A

HARD LIFE FOR ME. YOU HUMANS HAVE IT SO EASY WITH YOUR CAREFREE LIVES."

"Yes, yes," muttered Penelope. She still hadn't really managed to figure out the road, but she'd already grasped that it was pointless to argue with it. Then she started to think about what the road had said about the hay and the rainwater . . . "Yes, yes," she said again, and this time she couldn't help grinning. There was certainly more than enough hay around at this time of year. And she might be able to use some exploding creeper corms during her visit to her father . . .

"Well, in that case, I hope there will be a *lot* of rain after my trip to Blackslough on the sixth of July!" she giggled. She blew two red strands of hair out of her face and started to pedal uphill with renewed energy.

24 Preparations

Sometimes, luck—or chance, or whatever you want to call it—simply comes knocking at your door with no warning. Penelope couldn't believe it when she found out while they were eating their cake that Granny Elizabeth's rest cure was due to begin exactly one day before Penelope's planned excursion to Blackslough. Her mother was going to take G.E. to the health spa on the fifth of July, stay there overnight, and then travel back the next day, she said.

"It's a long way, so I won't be home till the next

evening. Would you like to ask Anna-Lea if you can go to her house for a sleepover, maybe? Or Tom, or Pete?"

"Mm-hmm," Penelope mombled with her mouth full, and knew in the same moment that of course she wasn't going to ask anyone. This couldn't have worked out better if she'd planned it! If her mother was going to be away on the fifth of July, that gave Penelope the perfect opportunity to sneak the ash paste out of her cupboard. She could turn her hair gray again, and then color it brown with her Icelandic Earth Brown dye, at her leisure. Even better, she'd be able to leave the house at the crack of dawn on the sixth of July without anyone being any the wiser.

Yes—she would carry out the mission to visit her father. And when her mother arrived home in the evening, Penelope would be home again too, and sitting in the kitchen as if nothing had happened. But something *would* have happened, of course—that would be only too clear on the seventh of July, because the postman wouldn't bring any sand-filled gray envelopes to the dragon house. Not on the seventh, and not on any other day—Penelope would have seen to that. She smiled contentedly.

The fifth of July was a week later. Mrs. Gardener and Penelope heaved Granny Elizabeth's suitcase down the steps and up the sand track. The taxi was already waiting by the beech tree to take her mother and grandmother to the station. Her mother gave Penelope a kiss on the cheek. "Say hello to Anna-Lea's parents from me, and make sure you thank them."

"Yes, Mom."

"And if I'm late getting back tomorrow evening, just go to bed, please."

"Yes, Mom."

Granny Elizabeth gave Penelope a kiss too. "Now, behave yourself while I'm away—I'm going to be gone for three weeks now, don't forget."

"Yes, Granny."

She lowered her voice theatrically while Penelope's mother helped load the luggage into the taxi. "And do some more reading in that lovely book so that we can have our ointment soon."

"Yes, Granny."

"And put this in your pocket," she continued, handing Penelope some money. "Get yourself an ice cream."

"Yes, Granny, and thanks."

At last Granny Elizabeth got into the taxi, and Penelope waved the two of them off until the car disappeared among the hills. Then she turned toward the dragon house and took a deep breath. The name "dragon house" didn't actually fit it so well anymore—so much of the green had flaked away from the splintered wood this summer that the house was barely speckled now—in fact, it was almost entirely red.

"You're red again, and soon I'll be gray again!" Penelope shouted to the house as she ran toward it, down the sand track, and up the steps.

She went into the kitchen, closed the door carefully, and made a beeline for her mother's wooden cabinet. Penelope enthusiastically opened the door, shoving aside some battered books and opening a large tin and two boxes in her search, and finally unwrapping a thick linen cloth from a tall, narrow jar. Bingo! The glass was slightly misted and quite heavy. The gloopy paste inside made a soft smacking sound as it lapped against the glass wall of the jar, fell back down, and started to crawl up again, like a trapped animal struggling to escape. Penelope unscrewed the lid carefully, and a familiar, biting smell of smoke rose to her nostrils.

Salon Penelope

It had taken six hours for Penelope's hair to absorb all the sticky paste. Now it was dry again, and every last strand was limp and as gray as dried cement.

"Ugh!" Penelope grimaced. "Horrible! How did I ever stand this? It feels disgusting."

It wasn't just the color she had a problem with—it was the way she felt inside: heavy and clumsy and dull. The lightness and permeability she felt with her natural hair had completely disappeared. She felt like half the girl she had been since the day her hair had turned red. In fact, she didn't feel like herself at all. But then she drew up in determination. “I’m Penelope Gardener, and I can handle this. At the end of the day, this is for my mom. She doesn’t deserve to get such nasty mail. I must get on and get ready.”

She opened the box of Icelandic Earth Brown dye; inside were a pair of plastic gloves, a small bottle of liquid, a tube of something, a sachet of shampoo, and an instruction leaflet that proudly claimed:

> Icelandic Earth Intense lends your hair maximum color intensity together with professional gray coverage.

Well, that was good to know. Now, where did it say how to use this funny stuff?

> Attention: An allergy test should always be performed before using this product.

I can’t do an allergy test now—I haven’t got time. Besides, this stuff can hardly be worse than the ash paste.

If you have just lightened or permed your hair, you should wait at least two weeks before you color it.

Hopefully that didn't apply to lightening with ash paste, as Penelope was even less able to wait for two weeks than to carry out an allergy test. Finally she came to the instructions, which said that the contents of the tube should be squeezed into the bottle of liquid, shaken well, and then distributed through the hair. Well, that sounded simple enough. In no time at all she had made up the color mixture and smeared it into her hair, and after half an hour, she could wash it out again. A quick blow-dry, and she was done.

A brown-haired Penelope looked out of the mirror, grinning. Very nice—no, wonderful! She'd never looked so normal in her life!

26 The Journey Begins

That night Penelope tossed and turned restlessly from one side of her bed to the other, tugging at her duvet and fluffing the pillow, but she couldn't sleep. Eventually, she sat up and looked out of the window into the darkness, then switched on the light and took out the old black-and-white photo of her parents. *Does my father still look the same?* she wondered. *Exactly the same, just slightly older?*

She lay down again and put her arms under her head. At some point, she fell into a light slumber that contained a confused dream: She was crawling through some sort of park with a gaunt red-haired man. The man pointed to a huge marble angel and asked: *"What makes you so sure that the key is under the angel?"*

"I dreamt it," the dream-Penelope replied, then gave a start because Coco's whiskers were tickling her face. Her temples throbbed, her body felt dull and fragile. It was already getting light outside. Oh, no, had she overslept? She glanced at her clock. No, she had another five minutes until the alarm.

She turned off the alarm, swung her feet out of bed, and dragged the rest of her body out after them. The floorboards creaked softly. Penelope stumbled to the bathroom, washed, dressed, and groped her way down the stairs sleepily.

She wasn't hungry this early in the morning, but she packed three thick cheese rolls with lettuce for later and filled a thermos flask with apple tea. She already had a big bottle of water in her backpack, but she hadn't packed that for drinking—it was to help her get high enough in the air when she left, and also to help the growth of the creeper corms along a little. The root was already in her backpack, of course, wound up into a bundle alongside a huge tube of superglue and Gina's Anti-Eye, and everything was padded with a thick clump of hay. Now all she needed was her purse.

Penelope was glad that Granny Elizabeth had given her some money before she'd left. She wouldn't have to pay for the bus to Senborough, as she could use her monthly bus pass, but she'd need money for her train fare to Little Pilling.

The first birds were beginning to sing as Penelope opened the door of the dragon house. The sky over the swamp forest was turning a faint greenish-yellow, and she could hear a cockerel crowing in the village. Coco pushed past her as she walked outside.

"Go back to sleep, Coco," Penelope suggested. "I'll be back this evening." But the cat wasn't having it. She followed Penelope to the bike shed and all the way up the sand track. When Penelope got on the bike and started pedaling, the cat tried to run after her.

"Coco, I can't take you with me! Go and catch yourself a mouse, or visit one of the cats in the village. You'll have a lot more fun doing that." Penelope waved to her and rode off.

The empty bus stop had a gloomy air despite the morning light and the dew shimmering on the buttercups. Normally other people waited here too, but at this time of day, they were all still in bed, of course. Penelope leaned her bike against a sturdy birch tree and sat down on the bench, her heart thumping from the exertion of cycling uphill.

"Bus, come soon, please. I need to get going quickly," she said under her breath, shuffling her feet restlessly. But the next arrival at the bus stop was not the bus; it was Coco, who had obviously followed her up the hill. The cat leapt onto Penelope's lap and nudged her head against her stomach.

"OK, OK." Penelope stroked Coco until she rolled herself into a gray circle, purring. The purring made Penelope feel good, giving her strength and driving the heavy feeling from her limbs.

When the bus arrived, Coco tried to get on, but

Penelope blocked her way. She couldn't spend the day keeping an eye on the cat. Anyone who has ever had to glue up all the postboxes in a strange village, give their unknown father a piece of their mind, and throw a lasso of creeper corms around his house, knows that a cat isn't exactly helpful for any of those things. But as the bus wound its way between the hills, taking Penelope farther and farther away from home, she started to wish she'd let Coco accompany her. She suddenly began to feel like she'd made a mistake, and this feeling grew until she was on the train, when she realized she hadn't thought everything through properly.

"Tickets from the last station, tickets, please." A round-faced conductor shuffled into the carriage, dragging his feet tiredly. The other two people who were sitting in the carriage pulled their tickets out.

"Good morning. I need to buy a ticket, please." Penelope rummaged for her purse.

"And where would the young lady like to go today?"

"To Little Pilling."

The conductor typed something into his ticket machine, then held a freshly printed ticket out to Penelope. "That'll be fourteen dollars and fourteen cents. That's lucky, that is."

Fourteen dollars? What was lucky about that? How could it be fourteen dollars? The journey was only an hour and a half, so why was it so expensive? Penelope could feel herself beginning to sweat.

"But, I, er, um, I . . . fourteen dollars? I've only got five."

"Oh, couldn't you have thought about that sooner, girl? Now I've got to cancel this and start again—have you any idea how complicated that is? Children, children, children. Of course you can't get all the way to Little Pilling on five dollars."

Penelope's heart faltered. She couldn't get to Little Pilling? What was the conductor talking about? She *had* to get to her father today, there were no two ways about it. She was already on the way now—if she had to get off earlier, how was she going to get the rest of the way to Blackslough? She could fly, but didn't know the way, and of course people would see her, and besides, she would have to use her water and then how would she get home?

"But, but, but that . . . I, uh." Her tongue began to click, and the conductor gave her a funny look. "Could you hold on a moment, please? I might have some more money in my backpack." She opened it up and looked inside. Hay, creeper corms, cheese rolls, water, tea, and the Anti-Eye.

She straightened up again. "How far can I get for five dollars?"

"To Synham. Five dollars and eighty-nine cents."

"I'll take that, then."

Penelope was relieved when she was finally holding a ticket in her hand and the conductor turned to a lady on the other side of the aisle who had lots of bags with her. At least now she could relax until the train got to Synham. After that—well, she'd just have to think of some other way of reaching Little Pilling.

The Anti-Eye

The lady with the bags got off at the next stop. Now the only other person in the carriage was a sullen-looking man sitting at the far end. *I'm sure he won't give me any trouble*, thought Penelope. She looked out of the window. The dusty meadows were scattered with hay bales, wind turbines, and colorless cows. Rusty railway parts lay in the brown grass beside the tracks, and there was a dead copse whose splintered remains of trees pointed like pale fingers into the sky. After a while, they passed a house with bricked-up windows and birch trees leaning on the collapsed roof.

Penelope felt a little uneasy. She knew she wasn't that far from home, but everything felt very strange and alien. She unwrapped one of the cheese rolls in her backpack, bit into it, and chewed. The conductor walked through the carriage again, grunted his "Tickets, please" again, and the next stop slid into view: a brick station, the stones more black than brick. After a minute, the train trundled on. Houses, fields, a rubbish tip around which gray-black crows circled, another train station. Penelope closed her eyes.

She fell into a deep and dreamless sleep.

"Next stop: SYNHAM," the loudspeaker clattered.

Penelope jerked awake as the sullen-faced man brushed her elbow on his way to the door. She glanced outside, dazed and disorientated—feeling as if she might easily fall asleep again. The man stepped out onto the platform. Nobody got in. Penelope read the station sign: *SYNHAM*. What? Oh, no! Suddenly, she was wide awake. She had no intention of leaving the train, but from now on, her ticket was no longer valid; she would need to be vigilant. In sudden inspiration, she fished the Anti-Eye out of her backpack. Snatches of an automatic announcement rang through the windows, and then the journey continued.

Penelope stood up and glanced up and down the empty carriage. Whatever else she did, she had to make sure to avoid the conductor. She pressed the open button on the door of the next carriage and peered inside, then quickly jerked her head back: The conductor was shuffling up the aisle, wheezing. *Quickly, Penelope! Back to your seat, backpack on your lap, ears open.* Now she just had to make sure she didn't get nervous and press the Anti-Eye too soon, otherwise she wouldn't get enough time, and he'd catch her. And, of course, she mustn't press it too late either.

The door of the carriage glided open. "Tickets from the last station, tickets, please." Penelope pressed her index finger hard on the small rusty button of the Anti-Eye and vanished instantly. Only a slight indentation in the upholstery where she was sitting marked her presence—and only the most observant person would spot that. As the conductor wasn't an observant person, he shuffled past Penelope's seat without even looking, and had left the carriage by the time Penelope reappeared.

She would have giggled in jubilation if not for the fact that the Anti-Eye had temporarily stolen her voice.

Penelope stepped off the train with a sigh of relief. The station here was small, like the previous stations, but slightly shabbier. A puddle-yellow stationhouse stood in front of the platform, its plaster crumbling, and a smeared ticket machine stood beside the gate. Two pigeons pecked at the concrete. Penelope checked the times of the trains running home—just in case she wasn't able to fly for some reason—and then set off.

A little later, she hesitated on the narrow road on the outskirts of Little Pilling and gazed over a harvested wheat field. She started to wonder whether this was the right way after all. There were no people in sight to ask for directions: The few watery-brown one-story houses with chain-link fences appeared to be deserted. She didn't really want to go ringing on doorbells, especially not so early in the morning.

Bam! Boom! A hefty shove from below set her catapulting forward. Penelope flew off the pavement and landed a good distance away into the stubble field. She nearly fell over, but managed to steady herself, holding her arms out for balance. "Thanks for the directions," she called to the road. Her voice had come back, at least. "But couldn't you have been a little bit gentler?"

No answer. That was always the case at this time of day, but it was a pity all the same—Penelope would have found it comforting to hear a familiar voice.

She started to cross the stubble field toward the forest.

28

Blackslough

The small forest Penelope was crossing had a bright and friendly feel. She inhaled the resinous scent of the trees as she walked, taking care to continue in a straight line as far as possible. It wasn't long before the little forest gave way to an embankment. Penelope paused and looked down the slope. Her heart leapt: She was here. Down there were the first houses. Down there was Blackslough.

Slipping more than walking, she made her way down the sparsely grown slope and followed the gravel road it led to, which took her to the outskirts of the village. There was no one to be seen except for a small Jack Russell terrier jumping up against a fence. Penelope felt in her pocket for the tube of superglue, hoping she'd be able to find and seal all the postboxes quickly, as her feet were aching. She hadn't had to walk very far, but her poor night's sleep combined with the newly dull and heavy feeling in her limbs meant she already felt exhausted. Chickens flocked in the narrow yard of a brick house nearby; then a large woman stepped out of the house and looked at Penelope in surprise.

Don't be a wuss, Penelope. Be brave—it'll save you a lot of running around, Penelope thought to herself. "Hello," she said to the woman. "Can you tell me where the nearest postbox is?"

The woman looked at Penelope appraisingly, as if she was deciding whether it was all right to speak to a girl who clearly wasn't from the village. Penelope smiled her friendliest smile and held the woman's gaze. The woman's drooping mouth quirked upward slightly.

"The nearest one's outside the post office. If you go round the bend and cross the road, you'll see a square on the right with the building society and the village shop. The post office is inside the shop, and there's a postbox right outside the front door." She turned away. Penelope thanked the woman—or rather, she thanked the front door, as the woman had already disappeared inside.

The little shop had a sign in the door—it wasn't opening for another hour. Well, that was OK—Penelope needed time to sabotage the postboxes. Beside the postbox right outside the shop, there was a transparent display case on the wall containing the community bulletin, the opening times of the town hall, and a map of the village. A red arrow on the map said, *You Are Here*, and the other arrows showed the locations of the primary school, church, picnic area, and so on. The map also revealed that Plasow Road had a public toilet, New Lane had a war memorial, and—Penelope couldn't believe her luck—Pond Place and Rose Street each had a postbox. She marched off.

"Wall Street" would have been a better name than "Rose Street," thought Penelope, as she passed the fifth stone wall as tall as a man. People around here obviously didn't like anyone looking into their yards, which was helpful for Penelope, as she didn't want people looking out from their yards and seeing her either. Otherwise they'd have seen a brown-haired girl unscrewing a giant tube of superglue, smearing the contents hastily into the letter slot, and firmly holding the flap on it. They would have seen the girl rattle the flap experimentally, the flap refusing to budge, and the girl smiling in satisfaction and triumphantly slipping away.

Well, Mr. Gardener wouldn't be posting any letters in the Rose Street postbox today, at any rate—and half an hour later, Penelope had seen to it that he wouldn't get anywhere with the Pond Place postbox either, or the one at the post office.

29

Waiting

Penelope stood in the village square on one leg. Then on tiptoe. Then on the other leg. She was bored. When would this stupid shop finally open? Surely it had been well over an hour since she'd read the sign! How long was she going to have to stand around in this square until her father came—or until anyone came at all? There probably weren't any customers in this Blackslough anyway, just walls and distrustful women feeding chickens.

"Practicing to be a dancer when you grow up, are you?"

Penelope jumped. A man with a mustache was leaning his bike against the wall of the shop.

"No . . . I . . . I'm just bored." Penelope's face reddened. She hadn't heard the man approaching.

"Bored—hmph! Wish I had time to be bored," the man muttered. A key clinked in his hand. He opened the bars on the door of the shop and disappeared inside. *Now we're in business*, thought Penelope. *The post office is open! The minute the first customer comes, full concentration.*

The first customer was an old lady with a walking stick. She was shuffling so slowly across the square that Penelope had plenty of time to observe her. Well, this obviously wasn't her father. She was a woman, for one thing—and besides, she was at least ninety, if not a hundred. She disappeared into the shop and emerged after a while with a newspaper and a small bag of sweets. Next came a mother with twins in a twin stroller, and then a bright red sports car drove up. A lady with short light blond hair stepped out, her stiletto heels clacking on the pavement as she tottered up to the postbox. She tried to open the flap, realized it was stuck, and disappeared into the shop.

Penelope's stomach rumbled. She was about to fish her second cheese roll out of her backpack when the woman in the high-heeled shoes emerged from the shop. Her phone was ringing. The woman was about the same age as Penelope's mother. Her red-painted fingernails gleamed in the sunlight as she pulled her phone out of her handbag. She glanced briefly at Penelope, then typed something into her phone before climbing back into her car and roaring off down the street.

Penelope's stomach suddenly plummeted as a possibility popped into her head: What if her father didn't turn up in person to post the letter? What if he'd sent his new lady friend instead? "Holy swamp cow! I'm such an idiot!" she said out loud to the empty square. Why hadn't she gone into the shop and watched to see who posted a gray envelope? If the blond lady had been the new Mrs. Gardener, posting a letter on behalf of her husband, then this whole trip had been a waste of time . . .

Her stomach growled again. Penelope fished out the second cheese roll, unwrapped it, and chewed it slowly. Between bites, her tongue clicked furiously. Her father's letter all those years ago had said that he'd met a woman who was "the same as him"—in which case . . . Penelope sighed in relief, brushing a strand of brown hair out of her face. "It couldn't have been the stiletto woman, because I didn't feel anything. No shivers across the back of my neck, no chills, nothing whatsoever," she murmured to herself. *Phew, I can relax again*, she thought. *I'm just going to have to be patient.*

30

The Man with the Fish Eyes

The Blackslough church clock struck twelve, and the midday sun beat down on the village square. Penelope sat in the inadequate shade of a maple tree, her eyes closed, feeling tired and heavy. Everything in her wanted to just lie down and go to sleep, right here on the paving stones. If her father didn't turn up soon, she was likely to sleep right through his arrival, despite any neck shivers!

Voices woke Penelope from a doze.

"A Coke, I'm allowed Coke now."

"Big deal. I've been allowed it for ages, you baby."

"I'm getting some sour snakes."

Running sandals on the road, laughter and shouting, colorful rucksacks, younger children tugging and shoving each other, and a teacher in a pale linen dress . . . Penelope watched through half-open eyes, as if through a haze. *Well, a school class definitely can't be my father, so I don't need to go into the shop just yet*, she thought blurrily, letting her eyes close again.

Whether she had heard the squealing tires first, or the car door closing, or whether the first thing she noticed was the fleeting tremor over her back of her neck and the shiver down her spine, Penelope could not say. *Someone like me, someone like me* . . . the words were beating out a rhythm in her head and her eyes snapped open for real.

Someone like me!

She jumped up. There he was, right in front of her!

Penelope recognized the person like her immediately. It wasn't exactly difficult: He was holding a familiar gray envelope. He was climbing out of a large silver car and wearing a smart suit. The T-shirt beneath his suit jacket was pale violet, and a black cloth was tied tightly around his head. Penelope guessed he was hiding red hair beneath the turban. He was approaching the postbox with a strutting gait like a cockerel's, reaching into his jacket pocket. He removed a spectacle case, flicked it open, and perched a pair of gold-rimmed sunglasses on his nose. *Where have I seen them before?* Penelope wondered, finding the sunglasses oddly familiar. He swept past Penelope and her heart leapt. She stared at his back and tried it out, mouthing the word "Dad." But it didn't feel right. It didn't fit, it didn't work somehow. Besides, she really didn't want to call him by that name, not when he'd sent them such vile letters.

Her father had arrived at the postbox and was trying to post the gray letter. He tugged at the flap but, of course, it was stuck.

"Dratted piece of rubbish! It's not working!" he spat, and went into the shop. Penelope followed.

It was deafeningly noisy, packed with the class of young schoolchildren Penelope had heard outside.

The man who might be Penelope's father joined the line at the counter.

"Dad." Penelope tried the word out again, but it rolled off the man as if he was a cold, slippery rock.

It's not him! The thought shot through her head, firm and true. *It can't be! No, it simply can't be! The fact that he's got a gray envelope in his hand doesn't mean a thing. Lots of people might send their post in envelopes like that. The gray envelope over there definitely isn't our one.* Penelope started to feel a little calmer. The man in the gray suit was simply someone of her own kind who happened to also be posting a gray envelope from Blackslough today. That was it. Yes, exactly. That had to be it.

If only I could see if the letter's got our address on it, then I'd know for sure! But that was impossible, as the man in the gray suit was walking up to the counter at that very moment and passing the letter over to the shopkeeper. Penelope would have needed eyes on stalks to be able to read the sticker on the envelope—or, even better, eyes on flexible telescopic rods. Although . . .

Behind what's behind, always lies what's before. You need the below, if above you wish to soar. The words resounded through her head as if from a long way off. *Hex videris, hex videris.*

A blinding flash shot through Penelope. She clapped her hand over her mouth to stop herself squealing aloud. She felt something dissolving inside her, or something separating, she couldn't be sure which of the two it was. The thing, whatever it was, seeped out of her and slid through a stream of air right through the students, invisible, moving farther and farther forward toward the counter. It drifted weightlessly under the man's gray soles, moved through them and into his feet, floated up his legs, then through his upper body, then through his neck, and finally into his head. Here it swirled gently back and forth, slowed its pace and finally settled behind the man's eyes.

All of a sudden, Penelope could see the man's blue-veined hand as clearly as if it was her own. She could see his hand holding the envelope, she could see the sticker with *To Lucia and Penelope Gardener* on it, and she could see the waiting face of the mustachioed shopkeeper behind the counter, as if she was standing directly opposite him.

The shopkeeper accepted the letter and popped it in a tray next to the counter. Penelope started to feel dizzy. She wanted to go back to her own eyes, her own body. She'd seen the envelope now, after all—but she couldn't break free, something was holding her, pulling her in. A dark place, a musty smell, greed, money . . .

"Aren't you feeling well?" The voice of the teacher in the linen dress broke through to her. She was leaning over Penelope's body and yet it was as if her voice were drifting down from far away. "Hey, are you OK?" The teacher touched Penelope on the shoulder, and when she didn't respond, shook her gently. Penelope felt the shaking, but she had to stay enveloped in that musty smell and find out what it meant . . . it felt important . . . she had to understand . . .

No! She didn't have to find out anything—not like this. She couldn't stay away from her body any longer; she had to return immediately. Otherwise, she knew instinctively, she would lose herself in another person's eyes.

Sssssssssssssskkkk! Violently, Penelope tore the "something" out of the man who might be her father. It jumped back into her own body, rough and fast. She coughed, her eyes flying open. Her head jerked uncontrollably to the side at the impact. She raised a hand and wiped her mouth.

"Are your parents here?" the teacher asked. "Or can I call someone for you?" Her face showed signs of relief that Penelope was awake, but she continued to frown in concern. Schoolchildren crowded around Penelope, curiously.

"Uh . . . thanks, but I'm OK," she stammered to the teacher, not really understanding what had happened. At that moment, the man at the counter turned around. He yanked off his sunglasses and raked his eyes across the small shop, a haunted expression on his face. His gaze ran over the teacher, Penelope, and the other children, focusing on each for a fraction of a second. His expression became one of incomprehension. His narrow eyes were gray and cold, the color of a dead fish. No, those weren't the eyes Penelope knew from her old black-and-white photo!

The fish-eyed man's lips moved slightly. His eyes scanned the crowd furiously once more, and finally came to rest on Penelope. For a moment, he hesitated, as if wondering if he was thinking the right thing; then he pushed his way through the children toward her . . . and grabbed the red-haired boy standing behind her by the arm. The boy gave a shout.

"What do you think you're doing? Let go of my student at once!" The teacher planted herself in front of the man, but he merely tightened his grip on the red-haired boy's arm. The boy had turned very pale. Penelope sat still, her heart in her mouth. She could tell from the lack of tingling that the red-haired boy wasn't magical at all—she guessed that while all magical people had red hair, not all red-haired people were magical! But why didn't the man realize the little boy was ordinary?

"I know it was you," the man growled, frowning. "It must have been, although you've hidden it somehow. How *dare* you? I'll show you how it feels . . ."

"You will not show anyone anything in here, Mr. Seller. Please leave my shop immediately," the shopkeeper shouted from the counter.

The fish-eyed man blinked.

"Did you hear me, Mr. Seller? Let go of that child immediately and leave my shop at once, or I will call the police!"

The shopkeeper came out from behind the counter and made his way through the terrified schoolchildren.

Seller was still glaring at the red-haired boy, but slowly his grip relaxed and he let go. "It was a mix-up," he growled suddenly, glancing around the room once more and shoving his way outside.

Penelope wished she could stay there safely in the shop, with the teacher, the shopkeeper, and all the children, but she knew she had to follow that guy. Right away. He had the wrong eyes, and he was called Seller, not Gardener. But he had the right letter, so he must have some connection to her father.

31

Pursuit

Outside, Seller was hurrying to his car. Penelope ducked behind a row of parked cars and watched him reverse from his parking space and drive across the square. She ran after him as fast as she could—but unfortunately that was not very fast, because the combination of her dyed, leaden hair and completing the *Hex videris* spell had totally exhausted her. The heaviness within her felt even heavier.

Luckily, a huge truck was blocking the silver car's exit from the square. Once she had caught up, it was easy for her to follow the car at a trot while the slow-moving truck trundled along in front of it. But the truck turned off a short distance afterward, and the engine of the silver car roared. It sped away, leaving Penelope following breathlessly.

"Oh, road! Please, road, I need to stay on that fish-eyed guy's tail!" she cried. "Please help me quickly, it won't be far."

The road didn't reply, and Penelope stamped on the road. "I know, I know—you have your own laws, and all of that . . . but if I don't get behind him right away, then . . . then . . . then . . ." She sank down onto the road. *"Please,"* she whispered, her lips almost touching the road. "Why won't you help me?"

"Spend a lot of time talking to the ground, do you?" A gangly boy wearing green sneakers brought his skateboard to a halt right next to Penelope's head. She looked up at him, feeling a little foolish.

"I've lost something."

"Money? Earring? Lipstick?" asked the boy, with a crooked grin.

"A car." Penelope stood up.

"Losin' a car's no biggie. Losin' a *board* would be a biggie."

"Well, that's a matter of opinion." Penelope had a thought. "You don't happen to know where a Mr. Seller lives, do you?" she asked. It was a small village, after all, and if it was anything like hers, then everyone knew everyone.

The grin on the boy's face vanished abruptly.

"*That* weirdo? Why are you asking? D'you know him or something?"

"No, but perhaps I'll be able to get to know him, if you tell me where he lives." Penelope tried to make her voice sound as casual as possible.

"He lives on Rose Street, in the very last house, next to this empty piece of land that's covered in weeds. But look, I'm telling you, I wouldn't want to get to know that guy—he's not quite right in the head. There's something rotten about him *and* the other guy in that house. If I was you . . ."

"You're not me, though," said Penelope. "And now excuse me, please, I've got to get going." She turned away—but suddenly it dawned on her what the boy had just said. The fish-eyed man lived with "the other guy"—that could be her father. Maybe he didn't bring his gray letters to the postbox himself, but had Mr. Fish-Eyes do it for him. She stopped and turned back to the skater boy.

"You said this Mr. Seller lives with another one like him. Does that person have red hair, by any chance?"

"Nah, it's not really any color—it's sort of colorless," said the boy.

"How do you mean? Has he got gray hair? A sort of ash gray?" asked Penelope, her heart racing.

"Yeah, sort of—you could call it a dirty gray, I s'pose. Whatever. Gotta go." The boy got onto his skateboard. "Good luck with those freaks. Perhaps they'll be a bit chattier than the ground." He skated off.

Penelope walked along the walls of Rose Street. At least she knew where she was going now, so she could afford to catch her breath and collect her thoughts. But it didn't matter, really: She was so excited that her heart was beating wildly, and her legs were longing to run in spite of their heaviness. She kept up a brisk pace and passed all the walls. Now she was crossing the overgrown plot of land the boy had described. Dark ivy grew over dank woodpiles, old barrels, and the remains of a rotten caravan. Stinging nettles, rusty stovepipes, small animal bones, cobwebs . . . she shuddered, walking faster.

Zuck! Zuck! As she approached the wall at the end of the wasteland, she felt two tremors on the back of her neck, tingling down her spine. It was a fleeting sensation, and very light, yet Penelope immediately sensed that there wasn't just one person of her kind around here: There were two. She could sense one person quite clearly—that was Seller—but the other was gentle, quiet. In spite of that, Penelope noticed that this second connection was completely different. It was familiar. It felt like a part of herself. "Dad," she murmured, and this time the word felt right.

Penelope shook her head, cross with the pang of longing and hope she had felt as she spoke the word.

She wasn't just here to meet her father; she was here to tell him to stop insulting them! She had to keep that in mind.

The wall surrounding the last house on the street was even higher than the previous one. It had nails and glass shards sticking out of the top, and Penelope could also see coils of barbed wire.

"Looks like you don't want anyone getting in here, Leo Gardener, you and your strange companion," Penelope said quietly. "If this is how you live, no wonder you don't have a problem with doing weird stuff like sending people sand in envelopes."

A massive steel gate loomed in the middle of the wall. *If only I could take a quick look behind that wall*, Penelope thought. It wouldn't be clever to peer through the gate—anyone in the house could see her then—so she snuck back to the overgrown plot. She squeezed past the decayed caravan and climbed onto a pile of wood, but even from up there she couldn't see over the wall. OK, then, she'd have to try something else. She quickly pulled her water bottle out of her rucksack. She rooted her feet—it was second nature by now—poured water over her head, and muttered, *"Semus triokko."*

Nothing happened.

"What's going on?" Penelope poured more water over her brown hair, jumped down from the pile of wood, and tried it from the ground. *"Semus triokko."* Nothing. *"Semus triokko! Semus triokko!"* Nothing!

Why can't I take off? Is this a dream? At least that would explain why it's not working. Exhausted and confused, she ran a hand through her wet brown hair.

The intense twitching rushed over her neck a second time, and a cold shiver ran down her spine. *Another one like me!* And then she heard a familiar noise—a loud, rumbling clatter.

Penelope peered out from behind the crumbled caravan and saw a tractor driving up the street: a huge green tractor with heavy twin tires. She'd seen it before, near the dragon house. It was the tractor that had tried to mow her down and, she was fairly sure, the tractor that had nearly killed her mother.

Suddenly, she remembered where she had seen Seller's gold-rimmed sunglasses—he'd been the driver! But he wasn't behind the wheel now. She clenched her fists. What was going on here? She knew what it looked like . . . but had her father really told these men to try to kill her and her mom?

She hurriedly ducked down as the tractor passed. The vehicle drove up to the steel gate. The man driving it drew a phone from the pocket of his black suit and tapped on its screen. The huge gate opened.

The tractor rattled inside, and the gates began to close slowly. Penelope didn't allow herself to think: In a flash, she whipped the Anti-Eye out of her backpack, ran through a bank of stinging nettles, pressed the button, and squeezed through the gate, invisible, at the last moment.

The tractor tires crunched over a path of white pebbles. Penelope jumped behind a large rosebush and watched the vehicle through the leaves.

32

Behind the Wall

A stately, cream-colored mansion stood at the end of the drive, a row of beautiful white columns lining the front porch. *Wow*, Penelope thought. *Even Pete's house isn't as luxurious as this!* She nearly rubbed her hands as she considered how much damage the creeper corms would inflict . . .

The tractor chugged to the house and stopped next to the sleek silver car, the engine cutting out. The man in the black suit climbed down awkwardly. When he reached the ground, he suddenly turned around and sniffed the air, like a wolf that had scented prey.

Penelope's breath caught in her throat. Had he sensed her somehow?

He can't feel me, she reassured herself, stroking her brown hair. *Nothing's going to happen; he can't feel me.* All the same, relief washed over her when the man turned away and disappeared between the columns. She noticed for the first time that the gravel path was lined with white statues. The marble figures sat, stood, or tiptoed on pedestals: She noticed delicate ladies in flowing robes, wreaths around their heads, and a huge angel with four wings carrying a child in its arms. *Strange lawn decorations*, thought Penelope. She remembered what the boy on the skateboard had said about the people who lived here, and felt suddenly afraid. Who were these men? What did they have to do with her father? And where was the woman for whom he had left Penelope and her mother? If this was the sort of company he kept, he might well be dangerous himself. Oh, why had she just slipped through the gate like that, without thinking it through?

“I’m Penelope Gardener, and I didn’t get this far by being afraid,” she whispered to herself firmly. But after a moment, she added, “But perhaps it’d be safer if I didn’t give my father a piece of my mind. I’m definitely planting the creeper corms, though; I owe myself that much. Close to the house, ideally, where they’ll do the most damage.”

She darted to the next bush, closer to the house, and waited a moment. Nothing happened. She ducked behind one of the statues—again, no alarm bells sounded, no shouts from inside. Penelope spotted a dense hedge a little farther down. If she followed it around, she’d find herself right up close to the rear of the house . . .

Behind the house, a number of marble statues had been tipped over at all angles, as if they had been knocked down in a struggle. They lay scattered in the grass around a black iron plate set in the ground next to the house’s wall—and they had lain there for some time by the looks of it, dirty and overgrown with moss.

Penelope's eye fell on a very small angel with broken wings and then on the black plate again. It was rather large—roughly the size of a door—and looked very heavy. Attached to the iron plate was a thick chain, which was wrapped around a large winch. Penelope bent the branches of an overhanging bush to get a better look at the black plate . . . oh, but it wasn't a plate at all—it was a hatch. *Is it a safe or something?* she wondered.

Just then she heard footsteps approaching. Her heart turned a somersault, her stomach contracting in fear. She dived behind the bush and curled herself as small as possible, clutching the Anti-Eye. The footsteps grew closer. From her hiding place Penelope could see two black-trousered legs and a pair of gleaming black shoes approaching through the grass—it was the second man, then, the one who had driven the tractor. He passed her without stopping, but she didn't dare breathe—she was sure the wearer of the shiny shoes would hear her.

A few moments later, she allowed herself a breath: There was such an almighty rattling and clattering that Penelope would have had to roar in order to be heard. *He must be opening the hatch*, she thought. She crawled along a little farther. There stood Tractor Man, sparse colorless hair clinging to his head in greasy strands. The heavy chain on the hatch was crunching around the winch, the hatch lifting squeakily.

Tractor Man leaned over the opening and smiled mockingly. “Gardener!”

Penelope jumped. *What?!*

“Wake up! It’s past noon!” Tractor Man’s voice was quiet, sharp and ice-cold. Penelope heard a voice coming from the cellar, but she couldn’t understand what it said. Tractor Man laughed for a moment, then whispered, “Seller’s already been to the post—your little letter is on its way. You were good last time, so this time there’s a little money for your family again. Never let it be said that we don’t keep our side of the bargain—that is, when you keep yours.” He ran a hand over his oily hair and spat into the grass. “You’re getting something cooked today, to keep your strength up—Seller's on it right now. I'll leave the hatch open a crack till he brings you the food so you can get a bit of fresh air. Aren't we looking after you well today, Gardener?" Despite his words, his tone was cold and mocking. His fingers cracked, and he turned a key in the metal winch box so that the hatch rattled down again, stopping just before it closed. Then he took the key out of the box and walked slowly back to the house.

Penelope squeezed herself into an even tighter ball behind the hedge, holding a hand over her mouth to stop herself from screaming or crying out loud. This couldn't be real—it was too terrible. It had to be a nightmare. She wanted to wake up. Wanted this to be over, for it not to be true. But she didn't wake up, she just lay there next to the strangers' house, hiding curled up on the ground, trying to deal with the fact that she knew who was sitting there, deep beneath the iron plate. A man called Gardener, whose family would get enough money again this month. Tears ran down her face. Her father had been imprisoned all these years, and she had done nothing to help!

33

The Cellar Spider's Transport

Penelope lay in shock on the grass behind the hedge, her arms wrapped tightly around her body, for a few long minutes. But eventually a faint noise nearby made her jump. She opened her tear-wet eyes. Right in front of her nose, a piece of dark green fabric with pink roses on it was sliding over the ground. Her mother's scarf.

What's going on? she wondered. The cloth jerked toward the big iron hole in the ground, stopping just short of the edge. A barely visible ripple passed through the fabric; then it turned slightly, and a gray-and-yellow cellar spider crept out from beneath it.

The creature crawled industriously toward the well and then moved as if it was lowering something very fine down the shaft—a thin string, thread, or hair. It looked straight at Penelope, then turned around, crawled back under the scarf, and dragged it forward until it, too, fell over the edge of the hatch and into the depths of the shaft.

A few moments later, she heard a voice. *Penelope, can you hear me? Please don't be scared.*

Of course Penelope was scared. She flinched, pressing the Anti-Eye reflexively. Who had just spoken? The voice had sounded like it was coming from inside her head, but it was a man's voice, not hers.

Penelope, I'm begging you, listen to me, said the voice. It was quiet and warm, and sounded fragile somehow. *This is Leo, your father. I know you don't know me, and I'm sure you must think I don't want to know you—you're bound to, after all these years. I can't explain what's been going on—well, not now, anyway. It'd take too long.*

Penelope stopped dead and listened, her heart beating loudly.

I didn't abandon you, Penelope. I'm being kept prisoner. I'm a long way away from you, but you might still be able to help me. All you have to do—you and Mom—is bring Coco to me. Please help me—bring Coco to Blackslough . . . bring Coco to Blackslough.

Then all was silent again.

Penelope was sweating. *Bring Coco to Blackslough.* She knew that phrase from somewhere . . . but where? The recollection wouldn't come to her. But what was she doing, wasting time thinking about that stupid sentence? There really wasn't time for that right now. She'd found her father, and now it was up to her to get him out. Now.

She crept over to the hatch. Hopefully no one was looking out of the window, as she couldn't press the Anti-Eye. If there was one thing she needed right now, it was her voice.

"Hello?" she whispered. "Hello, Dad, it's . . ."

"Who . . . who's that? Who's there?" The fragile, warm voice floated up to her and Penelope once again felt her spine tingle softly.

She took a deep breath. "Dad, it's me. It's Penelope."

There was complete silence below the iron hatch.

"Dad? Dad, what is it? Why aren't you saying anything?" She could hear him muttering down there, but could only make out odd phrases.

". . . can't be . . . Simon's only just brought me the hair . . . can't go that fast . . . all of his . . ."

"Dad, listen, I . . ."

"Penelope, is that really you? You've got to get out of here right away. It's dangerous!" her father shouted.

Penelope sighed. "I know. And that's exactly why I'm not going anywhere. I'm getting you out of there."

"Is Coco with you?"

"No, Coco isn't with me. Now please listen to me," said Penelope impatiently.

But her father wasn't listening. "Penelope, however you got here, you need to go straight back home and bring me the cat." His voice trembled. "She's my only hope . . . I'm begging you."

Penelope let out a sigh. Why was he so obsessed with Coco? She spoke very slowly and calmly, as if she was talking to a sick animal. "Coco isn't here, and I can't conjure her up out of thin air. But I've got a few other things with me that might be a lot more help than an old cat. You just need to do exactly what I tell you."

Her father groaned. "Penelope, you don't know what—" he began, but she ignored him.

"I'm going to throw down an Anti-Eye now."

"A what?"

"An Anti-Eye. It's just a little metal box, but it has great powers. If you press the rusty button on it, you'll become invisible. The only trouble is, the thing's not working properly, and the effect only lasts for ten seconds—oh, and you can't talk for a while afterward, but that wears off. So"—her father started to say something, but Penelope wouldn't let him speak—"when this Seller comes to bring you your food, you must press the Anti-Eye, OK?"

"How do you know about Seller?"

"That's not important right now! Look, I'm going to throw the thing down, and you need to press it, OK?" cried Penelope in exasperation.

"But what use is that supposed to be?"

Good grief. Was her father slow on the uptake, or hadn't she explained it clearly enough?

"With any luck, it'll be all the use in the world! Don't you get it? Look, pay attention: If old Fish-Eyes looks down the well and can't see you, he'll think you've escaped. He'll look down, and he won't believe his eyes at first, but then he'll rush off to tell his side-kick. He won't think to close the hatch, because he'll think you're not in there anymore."

Her father cleared his throat. "But Penelope, what then? I'm sitting here umpteen feet underground, how am I meant to get out? I haven't got the strength to float, and as far as I can sense, you're not one of us—uh, I mean, you can't . . . oh, I'm sorry, you, I, er—oh, nothing."

"Don't worry about getting up to the surface," said Penelope calmly. "I've sorted something out about that. You won't need to float." And then she said, not calmly at all: "And about the other thing—my kind, your kind, our kind—there are ways of masking it, you should know that better than anyone. If you . . ."

The gravel crunched.

"Someone's coming," hissed Penelope. "Catch!"

The Anti-Eye fell down the shaft, and because Penelope didn't hear any impact, she knew her father had caught it. Now all she had to do was quickly duck behind the hedge and mix the hay with the water.

34 Freedom

Seller walked straight past Penelope's hiding place, carrying a pan and a plate. Placing them both on the ground in front of the hatch, he stuck the key into the box and the chain started to rattle. When the hatch was half-open, he cried: "Gardener! Luncheon is served! Are you going to catch the pan, or shall I pour the soup on your head?"

The hatch rattled higher.

"You not answering today, then, Gardener?"

Now, thought Penelope, *now he'll look down. Press the Anti-Eye now, Dad.*

Fish-Eyes bent over the well with a snake-like movement. He froze.

"Gardener?! Where . . . ? Where . . . ?"

Penelope counted in the silence. The guy could look down for ten seconds, and not a second longer, otherwise it would all be over. *One, two, three, four . . .*

"Aaaaalaaaaarm! Serge! Alarm!" Seller turned on his heel and hurried to the house. The second he had passed Penelope, she raced out of her hiding place. Quick as lightning, she knotted one end of the long creeper corm root onto the winch, throwing the other end down to her father. She snatched up the bottle of hay water and poured the liquid carefully onto the creeper corm root. She hoped the road really had been speaking literally when she said it would explo—

Boom! Boom! Kra-woom!

The road hadn't been exaggerating! One corm after another swelled and ballooned until they hung in the darkness like a chain of fat coconuts, right down to the floor of Leo's prison, a sort of knitted ladder with oval rungs.

"Can you climb up?" Penelope called down.

A strange wordless whisper was all that came from her father, but Penelope wasn't worried: After all, he'd just pressed the Anti-Eye.

The creeper corms barely moved as Leo Gardener scrambled up to the surface. *How skinny he is*, thought Penelope, feeling sad and oddly shy. His bristly hair was dull, and his jeans and shirt were filthy and tattered, but he was definitely, 100 percent her father, and a grin spread over her face, unbidden.

"It's true, Serge! Damn and blast! He's gone. Will you just come here?!"

The roars of the fish-eyed man were getting nearer.

"Go on, then, do it! He can't be far away!"

Quick as a flash, Penelope untied the creeper corm root from the winch and threw it into the cellar.

"Simon Tschakerno," called Leo Gardener in a whisper. He placed his hand on the edge of the hatch, and the cellar spider crawled onto it. But as he leaned over the hatch, the Anti-Eye slipped out of Leo's breast pocket and plummeted down the shaft, right into the middle of the creeper corms.

"Come on!" hissed Penelope. They couldn't afford to worry about the Anti-Eye now! Together, they stumbled behind the hedge and threw themselves flat on the ground—and not a second too soon, as the two men now raced around the side of the house and toward the cellar hatch.

"What in the name of sanity is all this?!" Seller's face was white. "Wh-what *is* all this? Those things weren't there before—the well was empty—you've got to believe me, Serge!"

Tractor Man ran his hand over his oily hair. "Don't get your knickers in a twist, Seller. Gardener can't have gone anywhere—I can feel him, clear as day. Go on! Climb down! Go and find out what that thing is—I'll keep watch up here."

"*Me?* Why me? Why don't *you* climb down?"

"What's the problem?" hissed Tractor Man. He rubbed his patent-leather shoe on his trousers and moved closer to Seller. "*You're* the one who wanted him to do that job tomorrow. *You're* the one who let him grow his hair, and *you* measured it yesterday! You said he wasn't powerful enough to float! If I'd known you'd stuffed it up, I wouldn't have left the hatch open today by as much as a crack."

"How dare you suggest I stuffed up! I did it exactly the same way I've always done it!" Seller shouted indignantly, but he took a few steps away from Tractor Man.

"Then how come Gardener's nowhere to be seen and instead there's a mountain of roots as big as my head lying down there, eh? How come? His hair's too long, there's no other explanation for it. We let him get too much power back, and now he's having a bit of fun with us." Tractor Man stepped closer to Seller. "You get down there and I'll guard the gates—it's the only way out. Quickly!"

Seller said nothing. He looked down again at the creeper corms and narrowed his fish-eyes. After a moment, he tapped a code into his phone and an extendable ladder rattled from the top of the well down into its depths.

Tractor Man ran off toward the big steel gate.

Hurriedly, Seller climbed down toward the giant tubers. He shivered as he reached the bottom of the well; it was freezing down here. He took a step toward the still-growing roots and picked them up. *Thump!* The Anti-Eye fell between his feet.

"Well, well, what have we here?" he said, grabbing the small tin box. "Hmm, this is really . . . Serge! Serge! Come quickly. I've found something!"

A hint of enthusiasm passed over Seller's usually expressionless face. He had a passion for anything technology-related. For a moment, he forgot why he was there, and only had eyes for the silvery gadget in his hand. Without thinking, he pressed his finger down on the rusty button on top of the tin box . . .

"What have you found, Seller?" Tractor Man came back over the lawn and looked down the well. "Seller, where the heck—?" He glanced around in confusion.

Keep your hair on, Serge, I'm still down here, Seller tried to shout, but all that came from his lips was a soft *Sssspppt* noise. He pressed the button a few times, trying to make himself visible again, but that didn't work, of course. *Stupid piece of scrap metal!* he whispered soundlessly, and started to climb back up the ladder.

"Selleeeeeeerrr?! Come on, man, what's going on here?" Tractor Man looked all around him in panic, then jumped a foot in the air as his invisible, voiceless sidekick touched him on the arm.

The impact with the floor of the well had got the Anti-Eye working properly again—well, almost. The invisibility was working the way the box's creator had intended. It now made a person invisible for half an hour—and they returned in pieces: first the head, then the feet, with the rest of the body following afterward. But as Seller had pressed the Anti-Eye several times, he would remain invisible for several hours—and voiceless too, as that was the only thing that hadn't corrected itself.

35

In Flight

Penelope and her father stood pressed against a column at the far end of the yard, hardly daring to breathe—they couldn't hear the sounds of commotion and struggle any longer, and Penelope was worried that the two men had started searching for her father in earnest. A gentle breeze made the trailing ivy rustle over the high stone wall.

"We need to get over that," Leo whispered. He scanned the wall, checking for protruding stones that might serve as footholds, even though the top of the wall was a trap of barbed wire and broken glass.

He was desperate—but Penelope knew it was too dangerous. She turned her attention to the gravel drive leading toward the steel gate. *We'll have to go out that way*, she thought. But the gate was locked. Her eyes wandered over the lawn, over the moss, glided over the stone figures, before resting on the angel with the large wings. A blurry image swam through her head, a faded memory of a story. No, not a story—a dream—the dream she'd had that morning! The one where she was crawling through a park with a red-headed man . . . what was it that the man had asked her?

How do you know that the key is under the angel? Or something like that?

And Penelope had replied: *I dreamt it.*

Penelope glanced around the yard. Finding no sign of pursuit, she sprinted to the marble angel and reached instinctively into a narrow gap at the foot of the pedestal. A key on a black band. *Bingo.*

"Come on, Dad," she called to him softly.

He was gazing at her wonderingly. "How did you . . . ?"

"Never mind—come on!"

Together, they ran for the gate. The key slid into the lock, Penelope turned it, the lock clicked, she pushed the gate open. She slipped through, her father following wide-eyed, as if he couldn't quite believe it was real. She locked the gate, and together they raced down Rose Street, across the village square, past the town hall, past the post office and the shop, where people shot curious glances at the girl and the man tearing through their village. On and on they ran, over the narrow dirt road, up the embankment, and into the forest.

Completely exhausted, Penelope and her father stopped in a clearing full of blueberry bushes and gasped for air. Penelope felt heavier than ever, and her father was very weak, of course. They were lucky to have made it so far.

"We could slow down a bit now. They won't be able to sense us from this far away, and the trees will hide us too," said Leo Gardener, gasping for breath.

The Blackslough church clock struck three.

"No, we can't slow down." Penelope started running again. "The last train to Senborough leaves at quarter past three. We need to be on it!"

She was in such a hurry that she stumbled and fell. Her father offered her a hand, helping her to her feet—it felt funny and a little bit nice, holding her father's hand. And then they were off again, weaving through the trees and sprinting over the stubble field, along the dusty roads and past the yards with the chain-link fences. As they reached the station, the train was already there and they jumped into a jam-packed carriage. The doors closed, and they were off.

Penelope and her dad stood very close together, back to back, squeezed between strangers who couldn't escape their sweaty bodies but shot them plenty of disapproving glances. The train was as full this afternoon as it had been empty this morning; it wasn't even possible to turn around. They couldn't even look at each other! Even so, Penelope kept thinking, *My dad is right here!* and kept trying to glance at him over her shoulder. At least no conductor would be able to squeeze through this jam of people to check their nonexistent tickets!

As they were boarding the bus in Senborough, Penelope held her monthly ticket up like a protective shield and said to her dad, "Let me talk to the driver. I know him a little. Maybe he'll let you ride for free." She shot the driver a friendly smile, trying as best she could to cover up her dirty and ragged father as she did so. But the driver was looking over her shoulder, his eyes wide.

"Leo? Is that you?" he whispered, looking like he'd seen a ghost. "But . . . but . . . how . . . ? You're . . . I mean, I thought, errm, I thought you'd been dead for years?"

"Hello, Fred, nice to see you," said Mr. Gardener calmly. "No, I'm not dead. I'm very much alive, and I'd like to travel on your bus, if you'd be so kind."

The driver opened his mouth but didn't say anything. Her father continued: "Fred, as soon as I have time I will tell you what happened to me. But for today, I'm asking you if you'll do me a favor and let me ride this bus, even though I don't have any money for the fare."

The driver blinked, then sat up decisively. "Of course you can, Leo." He printed a ticket for Mr. Gardener. "Of course you can. What a question. As if I wouldn't give a lift to the best goalie our soccer team ever had."

Penelope looked up at her dad wonderingly as Mr. Gardener took the ticket, smiling. A group of teenagers rushed into the bus, and Penelope and her father were pushed toward the seats at the back. Jerkily the bus pulled away.

Penelope thought that if she wasn't already sitting down, she probably would've fallen over. She couldn't quite believe her father was here with her. She looked at him again, afraid he might dissolve into thin air at any second, like a dream in the morning. It simply couldn't be true, that he was actually sitting next to her on the bus!

Leo Tells All

"Dead? Why would I be dead?" Mr. Gardener wondered aloud. "Where would Fred get an idea like that?"

Penelope winced. She hadn't wanted to admit that her mother had been telling everyone—even Penelope!—that he was dead for a long time now. Her father looked so wretched as it was; he didn't need to hear that on top of everything else.

"It'll take Seller and Platell less than two days to reach our house," Leo broke into Penelope's reflections. "But as soon as Coco is with me, they won't stand a chance."

"What's Coco got to do with this? Why do you keep going on about Coco?" asked Penelope, a little irritably. *She* was the one that had rescued him, after all!

"Coco is my battery cat."

"Your *what*?"

"My battery cat." Leo laughed quietly. "Well, that's what I call her for fun, anyway. You know, I used to dye my hair with the ash paste—but I couldn't bear how heavy it made me feel. That stuff doesn't just make us undetectable to our kind, you know—I always found that it made me feel sluggish too. I couldn't even fly with the ash paste on my hair. I couldn't stand feeling that way—so unlike the way I usually felt. So before I put the paste on my hair, I always transferred a big chunk of my powers to Coco so that she could give them back to me as and when I needed them—whenever I stroked her, in fact. That's why I call her my battery cat, although Coco's never really liked that name."

The bus stopped in a new housing development, and quite a few of the teenagers got off. Penelope gazed through the window without really seeing them; she was too busy thinking about what her father had just said. How had she never realized that Coco was loaded with her father's power? It was so obvious, now that she knew. Whenever she stroked the cat, she always felt stronger, clearer, and calmer. And that very morning, at the bus stop, Coco had drawn the heaviness out of her limbs.

"The day I disappeared," said Leo, "Coco followed me into the forest, but I shooed her away. Perhaps that was stupid of me . . . perhaps none of it would have happened if I hadn't done that. All I remember is looking up into the crown of a tree . . . and then nothing. I don't remember anything after that. Something must've fallen on my head, something heavy—because when I came round, my head hurt so much that I was sick. It was dark around me—the ground I was lying on was hard, and I was freezing. Especially my head, because I was bald—I didn't have a single hair left."

Her father fell silent. He seemed to be fighting tears, Penelope thought, and he looked as though he might topple from his seat at any moment. She had to do something, say something . . .

"Mom will be happy to have you back," she whispered.

Her father's face relaxed a little, and a warm glow came into his eyes.

"Lucia, my Lucia," he said softly. But then he frowned, returning to his story. "I don't know how long they kept me prisoner before they talked to me. I didn't know where I was, I didn't know what was going on. Seller turned up at some point. He said if I used my powers to make money for him and Serge Platell, eventually he'd let me go. I didn't really have any choice but to comply. I'd known them both for a while, and I knew that they could hardly do anything themselves, but that they were quite violent. They waited until my hair had grown long enough again that I had the strength to carry out a job for them."

Penelope swallowed. She thought about how angry she'd been with her father, and she felt ashamed. "But they had powers, too, didn't they? Why didn't they just do all this themselves?"

"Everyone who is like us has a different type of power, Penelope—and not everyone is as strong as me. When I was young, getting into people's heads was my specialty. I thought it was funny to annoy people with it, and I could almost do it in my sleep. It didn't take much of my power at all," he said, with quite a bit of pride, but then his voice grew serious again. "They used me to influence business deals to their advantage. It was really clever. They grew rich and it looked entirely legitimate—but whatever money I helped them make, it was never enough. They threatened to harm you and Lucia if I didn't agree to their demands. So I agreed—but I persuaded them to at least let Lucia know I was alive and send money to the two of you every month, to cover your essentials."

Yes, and how charmingly they went about that, thought Penelope, sliding around restlessly in her seat. They'd sent her mother a forged letter . . . and this year they'd put her in the hospital too.

"But they knocked Mom down with their tractor!" she whispered.

"Yes, I know," said Leo bitterly. "My head visit in April didn't make them as much money as they wanted. The accident was their way of getting their own back."

"But if you had the power to get into other people's heads, why didn't you have enough power to free yourself?"

"Seller and Platell have known me since I was fourteen, since I took my first training course with Alpha Regius. We were never friends, but when you train together, you get to know each other very well. When I would meet with people like me, it was with them, among others—and we would share everything about our powers. So they knew exactly how long my hair needed to be for me to infiltrate someone else's head. They measured it regularly, and never let it grow too long between jobs. Besides, to really get into someone's mind, you have to look them in the eye very carefully. Or you need one of their possessions, something that's very important to them, something they like. Of course, Seller and Platell never looked me in the eye, and I didn't have anything that was important to them—maybe that's because nothing *is* important to them, except money."

The bus stopped again, this time in a village Penelope recognized. They weren't far from home now.

Leo took up the story again. "But a year ago I started to plan my escape."

"A year ago? What was so different about a year ago? Did they forget to cut your hair?"

"No, of course not. They're not that stupid. But something changed: A cellar spider fell into my otherwise sterile prison. He was called Simon Tschakerno. I had to take good care that Seller and Platell didn't stumble across him." He took the gray-and-yellow cellar spider out of his pocket and gazed at him fondly on the palm of his hand. The creature waggled its front legs at Penelope as if to say hello. "It wasn't easy getting into the little fellow's mind, but after a few weeks, I managed it. He let me a little way in, so I politely asked him if he could walk to my house to bring me something you loved. He went off, and came back after a few weeks with your blue shoelace."

"My blue shoelace? But I haven't got any blue shoelaces. I never have!" exclaimed Penelope.

"No? That's strange," mused her father. "I definitely got through to someone . . ."

"Oh!" Penelope realized suddenly. "They were my friend Pete's! That's why he heard your voice in his head!"

Penelope's dad smiled. "Simon told me you were wearing sneakers that were too big for you—I suppose I should've guessed they weren't yours. But Seller took the shoelace off me almost immediately. First Simon tried to bring me Lucia's scarf, the one with the roses on it, but that all went wrong. He managed to bring it most of the way through the swamp forest, but then someone picked it up."

Penelope bit her lip. "That was me," she said in a small voice, grimacing apologetically at the cellar spider. "I didn't know Simon was sitting under it."

"Well, why should you?" Leo looked at her affectionately, slipping Simon back into his pocket. "The amazing thing is, he only just came back today with Lucia's scarf and one of your hairs. I could never have guessed that you were virtually under my nose at the time. But how on earth did you manage to find me?"

37

Together

Penelope took her father's hand and slowly told him everything as the fields rolled past the bus window. She told him about the gray envelopes full of sand, about her anger, about her plan to dye her hair, plant creeper corms in his yard, and give him a piece of her mind. She told him how she had followed Seller, how she'd used the Anti-Eye to sneak behind the tractor, and how she'd crept along the hedge to the well where Leo was being held. She told him who had given her the wonderful Anti-Eye, too, about Gina.

Everything was flying out of her mouth in a torrent now. She told him how Granny Elizabeth had given her the Alpha Regius book, and that she could do hearing-before-hearing, that her tongue clicked, that it always rained on her birthday but the rain wasn't really wet, and that she could float—or rather, that she *had* been able to, but now it wasn't working anymore, which she thought was probably because of the ash paste.

She told him about the road, how it had saved her life, and that G.E. was on a rest cure at the moment and her mom was with her, and that her best friend with the blue shoelaces was called Pete, and that his father had been very rich, but soon wouldn't be anymore. She talked about the school trips and biology experiments, and homework and herb picking, about dreams and tears, bike rides and films, tooth gaps and bruised knees, about the time when she swallowed a pearl, about dancing, igloos, Christmas, thunderstorms, and how happy she was that he was back, and that he must never go away again . . .

Penelope couldn't stop talking. She wanted to speak on and on, and never stop. For more than ten years, she hadn't been able to say anything to her father, and now she wanted to catch up, to tell him every single thing she'd done in that time, everything she knew, and wanted to know. She wanted to explain, and tell, and share, and the tears began to run down her face, and she started to tremble, and . . .

Leo Gardener pulled her to him and held her tightly. "It's all right, Penny, my little one. I'm here now, and no one will ever separate us again."

He stroked her dyed-brown hair, and she grew calmer, breathing deeply. Silently, she pressed her head against his chest and listened to his heart beating firmly and evenly. Her nose dripped, and she fumbled for a tissue. The bus took a sharp bend.

"I need some refreshment after all that," she muttered to herself, opening her backpack. She split the last cheese roll, and passed half to her father. She poured apple tea into the thermos cup and sipped it. The tea was hot and mild and sweet.

When the bus reached their stop, Leo said goodbye to the driver and promised he'd be at soccer training again soon. Penelope started to unlock her bike, then paused suddenly. A faint tingling sensation was racing down her neck and spine. Suspicion spread within her, growing and swirling and finally becoming a certainty.

"They're already there," she whispered. "They're already at our house."

"What? Are you sure?" Leo tensed—and then paused, nodding as if he felt it too. "Then—then . . ."

Penelope saw fear in his eyes.

". . . then now we'll give them what for!" she finished his sentence. "You wait here, and I'll slip over to the dragon house—"

"Are you crazy? I'm not letting you go down there on your own!"

"But you have to," Penelope said calmly. "They'll be able to sense you. They won't be able to sense me because I'm wearing the gray paste. So I'm going to nip home, grab Coco, and meet you back here in twenty minutes at the latest. And then they'll really see some fire-red magic!" She grinned up at her father.

Leo Gardener hesitated, his expression torn between hope and uncertainty. Penelope could tell that he would have preferred a different plan; that he wished he was stronger, and wanted it to be him protecting his child, not the other way round. Penelope took his hand. "I'm Penelope Gardener and I'm your daughter. You don't need to worry about me. I've inherited a lot from you, and I'd like to learn a lot more—so I'm not going to let them take you from us again!"

He swallowed quickly and smiled, a little crookedly. At last he nodded, pulled Penelope to him, and kissed her on the forehead.

Penelope raced off down the hill—on foot, because she had to be stealthy. As the beech tree came into view, she climbed down the little embankment, then ran along parallel to the road, stooping down and camouflaged by the scrub.

Zuck! Zuck!

Penelope jumped. The tingling sensation was even clearer now. She had been right—they were already at the house. Cautiously, she peered through the leaves of the bushes and spotted the silver-gray car, partially hidden in a haystack next to the dragon house. *Do they think we're blind?* thought Penelope. Seller and Platell had covered the car so sloppily with the hay that even from a distance you could tell it was empty. She looked all around, but couldn't see anyone. Did that mean Seller and Platell were already in the house?

Penelope had reached the herb bushes. She crawled closer to the dragon house, remaining undercover. The front door was shut, as usual, and the windows were all undamaged—at least on this side. Where *were* those guys?

Suddenly, there was a rattle above the steps. Coco nudged her way through the cat flap in the front door and stuck her nose in the air. Penelope's heart gave a leap. *You good, smart cat*, she thought, feeling a warmth blossoming in her chest.

"Come here," she whispered, but Coco didn't seem to hear her. She remained where she was, her face tilted upward, sniffing the air.

"Come on, Coco, please," said Penelope, a little louder. The cat still didn't seem to hear her, but she came a few paces down the steps. Penelope crawled cautiously nearer. All of a sudden, Coco jumped, and started to retrace her footsteps back into the house. No, she couldn't! *No, Coco, not back inside!*

Penelope ran. Coco was halfway through the cat flap, when Penelope caught up with her and yanked her back outside. The cat mewed in protest, but Penelope pressed her to her chest. "It's all right, Coco." She turned to run down the sand track with the cat in her arms and slammed into thin air as if it were a stone wall.

The wall of air grabbed Penelope and spoke. "Well, well, who have we here?"

Seller! He was still invisible! Tractor Man emerged from the bike shed, a scornful sneer on his mouth.

"If we've got her," he said, "that means we've got Daddykins too."

At that moment, Coco raked her claws across Seller's invisible face—clearly he wasn't invisible to cats! Seller screamed loudly, and Penelope felt his grip loosen around her arm. She yanked herself free, leapt over the nearest bush, and raced across the meadow. She held the hissing cat in her arms and felt new strength flow through her.

Platell started after her. He was faster and gained on her quickly, his footsteps thumping in the meadow grass. He was reaching a hand out to grab her when Penelope whispered into Coco's ear: "Thank you for your power! He's at the bus stop." Then she let go of the cat and tore off toward the swamp forest.

38

Sunk

Running through a swamp forest wasn't exactly safe—Penelope knew that. But she didn't have much choice—and on the plus side, she was forcing Seller and Platell to run through the swamp forest too. She had to concentrate on sticking to the path. If she could just divert the pair of them for long enough . . . Coco wasn't exactly the fastest runner on the block anymore, especially up the steep hill to the bus stop.

At a moss-covered tree, the narrow path divided into two. Penelope raced for the left-hand fork, skidding on a slick of mud over a root. She heard laughter.

"Go on, run!" shouted Platell. "Yeah, run the lungs out of your body. You won't get away!" But his voice was a little distance behind, echoing through the trees, and Penelope realized she had built a decent lead. After another few moments, she risked a glance over her shoulder—but to her surprise, Platell had stopped running. He was walking. She didn't understand... but as he laughed out loud, and as Penelope glanced ahead again, she saw why: In the middle of the road stood Seller. Well, his shoes stood there, anyway—and his head was floating in the air.

Penelope stopped running and stood rooted to the spot. She was trapped.

Platell was walking over to her at a leisurely pace: He had all time in the world. His prey could no longer escape him, and Penelope could tell he was savoring every moment. She bit her lip, her heart hammering—half from the run and half from the fear flooding her body with adrenaline. No! She couldn't let herself be captured! If they had her, they could use her to blackmail her dad, and she just couldn't let that happen. Her father had suffered for long enough and she wouldn't allow him to suffer again.

She breathed out, and a deep peace washed over her. *My power's almost run out*, she realized, *but Coco left me a little. I hope it'll be enough.*

Seller's head was bobbing in her direction, and Platell had smug satisfaction written all over his face. Penelope stayed very still as they drew closer and closer, feeling the soles of her feet tingle. Before the men reached her, she whispered two words under her breath, then took a large step down from the path—straight onto the surface of the swamp.

And she didn't sink!

She ran, tearing along the surface of the swamp. Well, not exactly along the surface, but a millimeter over it—only the sharpest of eyes would have noticed that. Soon she had vanished from the pair's sight between ragged giant leaves, and was relieved when she reached firm ground and stopped. Running in the air had never been easy.

"Come on! After her, the ground's holding!" shouted

Platell, and the two men dashed after Penelope. The swamp slopped, the smacking noise resounding through the forest. Penelope watched through the leaves as Seller tried to turn back. Too late—they were already sinking! Platell rowed his arms comically, bending his body backward in an attempt to break free of the sucking mud . . . but the mire had them firmly in its clutches. Penelope knew the swamp mud would already be creeping under their clothes, cold and wet. And the more they thrashed, the deeper they sank. Platell was chest-deep, Seller right up to his invisible neck. Penelope frowned. If they didn't stop thrashing about, they might be in serious trouble! She turned and started to float carefully back toward the pair. The two men were screaming now. What should she do?

There was a rush of air above her. The treetops leaned gently to the side, and like a red dragon, Leo Gardener rushed downward and landed on the swamp at her side. He held his arms in the air, a dazzling light radiating from his hands. It was so bright that Penelope shielded her eyes with her arm.

"Mesoll vargerwno!" her father shouted, his voice deafening. The light rays were directed on the two heads in the swamp. The mud bubbled, there was a hissing sound, and then something seemed to rip, sending a glowing mud fountain shooting up to the treetops. Then all was quiet.

"Wonderful, really wonderful," chuckled Seller. Suddenly, he had a strong American accent!

"So this is Europe!" said Platell.

"Come along, Penelope," her father said quietly. "We need to call the swamp forest rescue service straightaway and let them know that two tourists are lost."

"What?" exclaimed Penelope incredulously. "But that's Seller and Platell!"

"That's as may be—but they now believe themselves to be Mr. Scott from Arkansas and Mr. Portway from Ohio, who are here on a relaxing break from their stressful businesses in the ironing board industry. European wellness excursions, swamp bathing inclusive. In Ohio they think of that as the ultimate in revitalization."

Penelope stared at her father. "What have you done with them?"

"I've let them forget."

"What?"

"I've let them forget who they are. 'Mr. Scott' and 'Mr. Portway' won't give me any trouble in future," said Leo. "And peace is what I need above all else, as I'm planning to spend a lot of time with my daughter and my wife." He smiled down at Penelope. "Come on, we need to ring for help before those two sink without a trace."

He took Penelope firmly by the hand, and together they made their way home.

39

Lucia and Leo

Dusk was falling by the time Lucia Gardener arrived at the dragon house. She was tired after the long journey from the coast and was looking forward to a long, hot shower and, of course, to seeing her daughter again. It was a warm evening and she wasn't surprised to see Penelope sitting on the porch steps—but what on earth had happened to her hair?

"Penelope? What's all this?" asked Mrs. Gardener, without so much as a "hello."

"My hair, you mean? It's called Icelandic Earth

Brown. I thought I'd try something new." Penelope smiled.

"But you can't just . . . I mean, you really should have discussed this with me beforehand," said Mrs. Gardener, vexed. She started to walk past Penelope.

"Stop! You can't go in yet. I need to talk to you first." Penelope stood up and barred her path.

"Penelope, please. I'm really not in the mood to play any of your little games right now. I've just traveled hundreds of miles and I'm absolutely shattered. And you're sitting here, you've dyed your hair brown without my permission, and now you don't even want to let me into the house. Would you like to tell me what's going on, please?"

"We've got a visitor."

"A visitor? Who?" Mrs. Gardener's expression was grim. A guest was the last thing she needed right now. Who, for goodness' sake, would be so impolite as to come so late in the evening—and without being invited at that?

"It's someone you know well, someone you like," began Penelope. "Please, Mom, sit down on the steps for a minute, will you?"

Finally, Mrs. Gardener surrendered. "OK, fine," she said wearily, and lowered herself beside Penelope.

"Actually, he's not really a visitor at all. He belongs to us. The person inside is someone who's very important to us. He's been separated from us for a long time, but not because he wanted to be—he was forced into it. There was nothing he could do. He wasn't the one who wrote that letter, and it wasn't him who was sending the gray envelopes either. He's been imprisoned and locked up all these years, Mom, and he's missed us desperately. But today he managed to escape. Dad's back. He's here with us again."

Mrs. Gardener stared at her daughter, scarcely able to take in what Penelope was saying. But Penelope was looking back at her with a peculiar, piercing expression, and her eyes were shining.

"Go in, Mom. Dad's waiting for you. Only, don't be frightened—he's looking pretty thin." Penelope stood up and put her hand on the door latch.

Mrs. Gardener stood up, too, but made no move to go into the house. She opened her mouth, her jaw trembling, breathing fast.

"But he was . . . I mean, he . . . he . . ."

Penelope shook her head wordlessly, and her mother pressed her lips together. She looked at the sky, she looked at the trees of the swamp forest, she looked into Penelope's eyes again. Then she nodded slightly, took the latch out of her daughter's hand, and opened the door.

Penelope blew her cheeks out and sat back down on the steps. She looked up at the evening sky too; the blue dusk was descending quickly, and a bright star hovered over the swamp forest. The cat flap rattled. Coco marched outside and nudged Penelope's stomach with her nose. Penelope stroked her soft gray fur.

"Isn't there anything for you to eat in there?" she asked. "Come on, let's go for a little walk. I need to go and get my bike."

Penelope and Coco wandered up to the bus stop together. Suddenly, there was a soft jingling sound, as though someone was jolting over the paving slabs on a bicycle. Penelope looked up. At the top of the hill, she saw a handlebar blinking in the twilight; then the rest of her bicycle rolled into view. It rode up to her, completely on its own, with only the slightest of wobbles.

"AFTER A DAY LIKE THAT, YOU SHOULDN'T HAVE TO STRUGGLE UP THE HILL AGAIN," the road rumbled, bringing the bike to a standstill in front of Penelope.

"Thank you." Penelope took hold of the bike just in time to stop it tipping over. "So you're speaking to me again?"

"I'VE BEEN SPEAKING TO YOU ALL THIS TIME, BUT YOU DIDN'T SEEM TO BE INTERESTED. I'M GLAD YOU'VE COME TO YOUR SENSES AGAIN."

"Oh!" exclaimed Penelope indignantly. "So now it's *my* fault?"

"WELL, IF I WAS TO COLOR MY TAR, PERHAPS I WOULDN'T BE ABLE TO HEAR THINGS ANYMORE EITHER," boomed the road. "AND I HAVEN'T GOT A CAT TO HELP ME OUT IF I GET INTO HOT WATER. AND NOW I BID YOU GOOD NIGHT." The voice faded to a distant echo, then fell silent.

"GOOOOOD NIGHT TO YOU TOOOOOO," Penelope boomed back. She laid her sweater in the basket of her bike, lifted Coco into it, and pushed to the sand track, then down to the house. She was so tired that she almost fell asleep midstep, but at the same time, she felt vibrantly alive and full of joy as she lifted the latch to go indoors, where both her parents were waiting for her.

40

Read All About It!

The newspaper headline should have read: *Sunshine on August 13—the sensation of the year!* But since hardly anyone had ever noticed that the rain on Penelope's birthday wasn't really wet, there probably weren't all that many people who were interested in the fact that it was sunny the day she turned eleven.

Apart from Penelope, of course.

"Yes! Yes, yes, yesssss!" She grabbed her mother's hand and pulled her out into the yard. Together they ran through the grass, and Penelope climbed the pear tree. "There's no rain today. And I'm eleven. I'm eleven,

eleven, eleven!" She plucked one of the unripe pears and threw it at her father, who was just coming out of the dragon house. "What's up, Dad? Aren't you excited? Would you rather it was raining, like it normally does on my birthday?" Penelope shouted, throwing three more pears in his direction.

Leo caught them one by one, biting into one of them, which had suddenly turned ripe in his hands. "Yes, yes. I'm glad," he said, but he looked a little bit embarrassed.

"Well, why do you look like you've eaten a thistle, then?" Penelope asked.

"Well, because I'm pretty sure I'm to blame for the weather on your previous birthdays."

Penelope jumped down from the tree. "That's rubbish! Why should you be to blame for that? You haven't been here all these years."

Leo nodded slowly. He sat down on the wooden steps. "That's just it. On the thirteenth of August every year, I thought of you. Every year I wondered how much you'd grown, how you were, and what you were doing. Whether you'd inherited my red hair—and the other thing too. I thought about you and wished I could be with you. That I could take you in my arms and twirl you around. That I could say, *Look, Lucia, my darling, look at our Penny—she's eight already, she's nine, she's ten.*

"When someone like us thinks so strongly about another person, it sometimes results in a thunderstorm around that person. But since I was sitting in that dungeon, and hardly had any strength, there probably wasn't even a storm—just that strange rain."

Penelope sat down next to him on the steps. She patted his knee. "Well, at least I never got wet from your rain. You know what? I think I'm going to lock myself into Mr. Ritter's old goat barn, and think of you very hard, and then we'll see what falls down on you, shall we?" She snickered.

"I think our daughter's just a little too sassy, Lucia. Don't you think so?"

"I think we should eat our breakfast birthday cake soon, that's what I think. There won't be any leftovers once Tom and Pete get here," said Mrs. Gardener, putting an arm around her husband.

"But I could always make another one," Granny Elizabeth, who was now outside too, said generously.

"Aww, thank you, Granny! But I'm pretty sure Gina will bring some fantastic treats from town this afternoon, when she comes for the party," Penelope said quickly.

"OK," said G.E., rubbing her old hands with some of the extra-special healing salve Penelope and her dad had cooked up. "Let's just hope she brings something better than the last time she was here. That so-called ice cream she tried to conjure up was nothing but colorless mush."

Penelope giggled as a bubble of excitement rose in her belly. Another thing had occurred to her: Now that she was finally eleven, she'd be able to start studying with Alpha Regius soon, like Gina's brother!

Penelope's birthday party that afternoon was the most fun that she'd ever had. She didn't know exactly why, but she laughed almost all the way through it. It was nice that Tom and Pete got along so well with Gina. It was nice when her mother played the clarinet for them too. And it was even nice when Granny Elizabeth showed them her collection of coins and explained them all, down to the tiniest detail.

Later that evening, when the birthday guests had left, Penelope sat at the kitchen table with her father, her cheeks flushed, smiling happily. G.E. and her mother were asleep, and Penelope was dog-tired too, but she wanted to have a look through the newspaper. Pete had told her there was a long piece in it today about the strange downturn, and the equally strange recovery, of the Intermix concrete mixer factory, owned by his father. Penelope was absolutely certain that Leo's captors had had something to do with the terrible business arrangements that had led to the downturn in the first place! As she skimmed over the article, she noticed something else: a report about the local soccer club. For weeks now, they'd done nothing but score goals, and hadn't let a single one in.

But the best bit was the article about a new species of giant red-headed bird! Penelope wanted to read that one too, but instead her eye fell on another story. A very brief one, under the category of "Miscellaneous News."

Giant Vegetables Blast Out Bunker

> A subterranean vault was blown up yesterday in a small community in the Plasow district. Experts assume that the explosion was caused by a strain of oversized pumpkin that was being stored in the vault. The explosion devastated the entire property, including the house. No one had been seen there by locals of the village for several weeks.

"Look, Dad. Perhaps we should call and tell them that the inhabitants are wandering around in Arkansas and Ohio now."

Her father looked thoughtfully at the newspaper report.

"Yes, perhaps we could," he said, but he didn't sound especially convinced. He ran his hand over the kitchen table. "I shouldn't have done that—made them forget, I mean." His hand stilled. "I just couldn't think of any better way to protect us. All I can hope is that things worked out for Seller and Platell, with their ironing board businesses. Perhaps they're living happier lives now."

Penelope frowned. "You wish them happiness after everything they did to you? You don't wish them any ill at all?"

"No, I don't," said Leo softly. "What would I gain from that? I'm just happy that I can be here with you today—with my beloved wife and daughter."

"But that's exactly why those awful men don't deserve a happy life!"

"Maybe," her father said quietly. "But it would be something new for them. They haven't known much happiness—everything was always about money. It never made them happy, and there was never enough.

I just want Seller and Platell to find something they truly enjoy."

Penelope went to the sink and drank some cold water straight from the tap. She didn't understand how her father could think that way, after everything he'd been through. But maybe she didn't have to understand.

Her eye fell on the newspaper again. "Oh, I wanted to read the rest of that."

"Not tonight. It's late," her father said.

"Are you kidding? Are you actually serious?! I'm *eleven* now—I can stay up half the night!"

"I suppose so," Leo sighed, "but I really wanted to read it myself."

Penelope puffed out her cheeks, reaching for the paper. But Leo was quicker. "Now, just you wait one minute, fire girl." He rolled the newspaper up and swished it through the air like a sword. "You want to steal your father's reading matter? Well, get ready for this, then!" With a sweeping, skillful stroke, he drove

Penelope squealing around the table and toward the stairs.

Penelope giggled, dodging him as best as she could, but her father pushed her ruthlessly up the stairs. She had no chance. She reluctantly took a bath, brushed her teeth, and put on her pajamas. She really was pretty tired. When she finally left the bathroom, her father was sitting at the kitchen table. He was drinking elderberry water and had his reading glasses on, and his head was tilted over the newspaper.

Penelope's fingertips itched. She couldn't help herself—she took a breath and whispered some newly learned words: *"Serfix dalons!"*

In a matter of seconds, the newspaper had folded itself up, danced briefly around her father's head like an excited chicken, and hopped up the stairs two at a time. Penelope snatched it out of the air.

"Hey!" her father said.

Penelope raced into her room, threw herself on the bed, and hid under the blanket. Already she could hear her father's footsteps on the stairs, and she knew he'd soon come through the door. Everything inside her chuckled and giggled.

I wouldn't want to swap my life with anyone's, she thought. *I'm Penelope Gardener and I am the best newspaper thief in the world. I live in the dragon house, and I have a battery cat. I've got my darling mom, and* G.E., and *Tom and Pete and Gina. I've got the road and my flying, and a book by Alpha Regius. I'm eleven, and I've got my father back.*